LOVE'S QUEST

Young widow Fleur Weston starts a new life when she turns her mother's legacy, Manoir de Belvoir, into a successful hotel and restaurant. Fleur and her small daughter love their French life, but the Manoir holds dark secrets: the sealed cellar in the Chapel; the young Remondin bride's grave in the grounds; and handsome American Jake Merton is also an enigma. Does he truly love Fleur, or is he too, only interested in possessing the Manoir . . .

JOYCE JOHNSON

LOVE'S QUEST

Complete and Unabridged

LINFORD
Leicester

First published in Great Britain in 2009

First Linford Edition
published 2009

British Library CIP Data

Johnson, Joyce, *1931 –*
   Love's quest.- -
   (Linford romance library)
   1. Widows- -Fiction. 2. Hotelkeepers- -
   France- -Fiction. 3. Americans- -France- -
   Fiction. 4. Love stories.
   5. Large type books.
   I. Title II. Series
   823.9'14–dc22

ISBN 978–1–84782–946–7

Published by
F. A. Thorpe (Publishing)
Anstey, Leicestershire

Set by Words & Graphics Ltd.
Anstey, Leicestershire
Printed and bound in Great Britain by
T. J. International Ltd., Padstow, Cornwall

This book is printed on acid-free paper

Fleur Makes A Decision

Fleur Weston, phone clamped to her ear, anxiously scanned the street below her third floor flat; streams of cars, scurrying figures hurrying to work, buses, bikes . . . but no Wanda. She checked her phone and redialled Wanda's number. 'Where are you?' she breathed. 'Please answer, I'm going to be late — again . . . '

Daisy Weston, Fleur's three-year-old daughter, banged her spoon rhythmically, dipped it into her dish and splashed soggy cereal all over the table, crowing with pleasure at the sticky mess. 'Wanda?' she said, looking hopefully at her mother.

'I hope so, Daisy, love, but she's not picking up her phone.'

Polish Wanda was a good nanny and

Daisy loved her, but since Stefan, Wanda's boyfriend, had arrived from Poland, her time-keeping had become a touch erratic. Fleur sighed. She didn't relish having to find another nanny. Wanda had settled in so well, was more friend than employee, but if needs must . . . She looked at the clock — twenty minutes late already. There was no option. She dialled her friend, Jane's, number.

Daisy climbed down from her seat, still waving her sticky spoon. 'Wanda,' she insisted, tugging at her mother's skirt.

'Doesn't look like it, love, and I can't wait any longer.'

'WANDAAAA,' yelled Daisy.

'Hush, pet, I can't hear. Jane . . . '

'WAA . . . '

'Shush, shush.' Fleur bent down and hoiked her little daughter on to her hip, hugging her close. 'Just let me talk to Jane, pet,' she soothed, as Daisy's sobs gathered volume.

'Fleur, what's the matter? Is Daisy poorly?'

'No, no, it's just . . . Wanda's not here yet and I'm late already.'

'OK, cavalry at the ready, bring Daisy up, she can come to playgroup with Alice. Better still, Sam's not left for work yet, so I'll nip down and pick her up.'

'Oh Jane, thank you so much . . . I'm so sorry . . . I . . . '

'Never mind that. I'm on my way. You ready for the off?'

'Yes, more or less. Two minutes . . . '

'See you in a sec.'

Daisy let out another roar of protest as Fleur eased her down on to the floor.

'OK, it's all right, Jane's coming with Alice.' She wiped the tears from her daughter's cheeks then quickly checked her own appearance. She was a disaster area; hair all over the place, bits of gooey cereal on her smart navy jacket, anxious dark-shadowed eyes. She'd worked on her laptop so late the previous night her brain felt fogged.

She scrubbed at the cereal with a damp tissue and tried to smooth her dark hair into some semblance of order.

Fleur's friend, Jane, who lived in the flat upstairs, arrived at the door. Alice, her daughter, was a year or so older than Daisy, who adored her. 'Hi Daisy.' Jane knelt to the still sniffling child. 'You're coming with us to playgroup! You liked it last time, didn't you?'

'And the time before . . . and before,' Fleur said. 'I'm so sorry, Jane. I'll enrol her properly in a few months.'

'You'll need to put her name down now, they're pretty full.'

'Really?' Fleur groaned, 'I hadn't thought . . . '

'Never mind. I'll check it out with the owner, put in a good word.'

'Sorry . . . '

'Stop apologising. We're fine and you'll be for the chop if your boss finds you late again.'

'Look, Jane, thanks for this. I know Wanda will turn up soon. She can pick up Daisy and Alice later.'

'We'll see,' Jane said doubtfully. 'Now go, we'll talk later. Come to supper.

Sam and I have something to tell you.'

'Really? Sounds mysterious! I'd love to come, depending on Wanda, of course.'

'Of course. Now GO!' Jane gave her friend a gentle push towards the apartment block's lifts.

* * *

The morning rush-hour journey into London was the usual nightmare. Crammed into a packed Tube compartment Fleur hung on to the nearest handhold, then struggled to the door to be decanted on to the platform and swept towards the escalators and up to the bright, early spring sunlight of London's streets.

Her office block was only minutes away. Already late, her only hope was to slide into the office unnoticed by her boss. As the sun struggled through the crowds on the thronged pavements she took a deep, steadying breath, lifted her face to the sun and hoped for the best.

But on this particular morning, luck deserted her.

Mr Edward Simkins, co-founder and senior partner at Simkins & Bartlett's Financial Services, chose this morning to check on his employees' time keeping. He pounced as Fleur came through the door. 'Ah, Mrs Weston, a word please.'

'So sorry, Mr Simkins . . . ' Fleur's thoughts whirled, seeking a plausible excuse: traffic accident, Tube explosion; lightning strike . . . 'Er . . . the nanny, she . . . ' and instantly realised her mistake. Mr Simkins, long past retirement age but, to the frustration of his younger executives, still clinging on to power, would not accept the non-appearance of a nanny as an excuse for being late for work.

He frowned. 'This is not the first time, is it, Mrs Weston?'

'No, but . . . '

'It won't do, Mrs Weston.'

'Mr Simkins, I took work home last night . . . and other nights. I'm never behind with my clients' business.'

'Hmm . . . and this . . . nanny. She lives in?'

'No. She comes in on a daily basis. Sometimes she stays over. She cares for Daisy — my daughter.'

'Ah. Is there a Mr Weston?' Mr Simkins ventured.

In spite of herself, a familiar dead weight of grief descended and Fleur felt tears threatening. She clenched her fists and said, 'No . . . I'm a widow.'

'Oh. I'm sorry. So sorry.'

'He, Ben, died over two years ago. In a car accident.'

'I'm so sorry Mrs Weston.' Mr Simkins looked at his feet, then at Fleur. 'I can see that must be very difficult for you. Any family nearby?'

Fleur shook her head. 'But Mr Simkins, I'm not looking for special treatment. I want to work here and I'm good at my job.'

'Yes. Ah well, try your best Mrs . . . er . . . Fleur. You know, the time-keeping.'

'I'll certainly do my very best. I am a hard worker and I'll do my utmost not to let it happen again, but as a single mother, I honestly can't possibly guarantee it one hundred percent.

'My family, my little girl, she has to be my priority. If that's difficult to reconcile with your business principles . . . ' In her head she said, 'I'll resign,' but she wasn't so foolhardy as to offer it. He might just take her up on it.

'No, no, not difficult at all.' In Mr Simkin's head was a potentially uncomfortable session with an employment tribunal. 'Just . . . um . . . try to do the best you can.' And, to Fleur's great relief, he turned and walked away.

Quietly, Fleur slid into her work routine, but her encounter with Mr Simkins had shaken her, and had prodded the dark and painful sore of widowhood. Desperately she tried to harness her thoughts and concentrate on her computer screen. She had a stack of clients and had responsibility for their financial affairs.

★　★　★

'Fleur?' Hazel, her friend and colleague touched her shoulder. 'Lunch?'

Fleur shook her head. 'I was late this morning, so it might be advisable to skip lunch.'

'We'll just have coffee, then.'

'All right.'

Over a cappuccino, Fleur unburdened herself to her friend.

'Maybe you try too hard,' Hazel said. 'It's difficult to find a work and family balance, especially on your own.'

'You do it. With three kids!'

'I have Mum and my older sister nearby. Have you . . . is there . . . ?'

'Anyone else? No. Ben's a hard act to follow.'

'What about whatshisname? Tom? Didn't he take you out last week?'

Fleur laughed. 'It was hardly a hot date, we went to the local DIY. Anyway,

I've known Tom since primary school. I needed some bedroom flatpack for Daisy's room and he came with me, that's all. We did have coffee afterwards, though. Tom's nice, a good friend of long standing but that's all there is to it.'

Fleur stood up. 'Look, I'd better get back, I promised Mr Simkins I'd be a model employee.'

'You do enjoy your job, though, don't you, Fleur?' Hazel asked.

Fleur sighed. 'I don't know, sometimes it's a burden, but I have to work for Daisy's sake, and I do need the money. But come to think of it, because of work, Daisy doesn't get much Mum either. I do believe my nanny, Wanda is the most important person in my daughter's life at the moment. Isn't that awful?'

'It's just the way things are. But look, why don't you bring Daisy over for a barbecue next weekend? It'll the first of the season!'

'Oh, Hazel, that does sound tempting. Yes, Daisy and I would love to come.'

The rest of the day dragged and Fleur stayed late to clear her desk so she could have a free evening for a change. Before she left, she rang Jane.

'Hope you're still on for supper, Fleur,' Jane said. 'Wanda picked the girls up and says she's staying on to make up for being late.'

'Oh. I'm still working. I'll be a bit late.'

'That's OK. We want to talk to you and, oh yes, there was someone today looking for . . .'

She broke off abruptly and Fleur heard Jane's husband, Sam's voice. 'Not now Jane . . . might worry her . . . wait . . . this evening . . . nothing wrong with . . .'

'What? What is it? Daisy?'

'She's fine, having a great time with Wanda, who, apart from her time-keeping, is an absolute gem. See you soon,' Jane said brightly.

Intrigued by Sam's comments, Fleur

couldn't settle back to work and an hour later she decisively closed down her computer and left the now deserted office building.

★ ★ ★

'Mum, Mum!' Daisy threw herself at Fleur as soon as she appeared at the front door.

'Daisy love. Did you have a nice time with Wanda?'

'Yes, and Steffi.'

'Stefan?'

'Mmm, Steffi.' Daisy clapped her hands and laughed.

'Fleur, I hope you don't mind,' Wanda said. 'Stefan called at tea-time. He had some news and couldn't wait to tell me. He didn't stay long, just had a cup of tea and played a game with Daisy.'

'I've told you, Wanda, he's welcome anytime. Not to ... er ... stay overnight,' she amended hastily. There were enough complications in her life without the nanny's boyfriend moving in.

'Course not,' Wanda said. 'He shares a flat with friends.'

'Oh, that's good,' Fleur said lamely. She had met Stefan and found him perfectly charming.

'I make you some tea,' Wanda said. 'Daisy had poached egg, jelly and fruit. Now she is tired, I think.'

Indeed, snuggled up to Fleur on the sofa, Daisy's eyelids were drooping.

'I bath her,' Wanda said.

'All right. Can you stay on a bit? Jane's asked me to supper. She has something to tell me, she says.'

'And I too, but not until tomorrow. I stay overnight, make up for this morning. Come little one, say good-night to Mummy.'

Fleur kissed her daughter. 'See you later,' she whispered.

She leaned back and closed her eyes. The flat was small but functional and she and Ben had bought it before rocketing prices put it beyond first-time buyers. If Ben had lived, they'd be looking to move. She could hear his voice now. 'Next step will be green fields, space, kids, dogs, garden . . . '

Fleur clapped her hands to her ears. 'No, Ben love, you have to go away. I can't bear it.' Quickly, she got up and went to have a shower, standing under the hot, stinging spray until her head cleared. Then, dressed in loose trousers, cream top, hair hanging free, she felt marginally better. She peeped into Daisy's tiny bedroom.

Wanda held up her hand. 'She's fast asleep.'

Fleur bent to kiss her daughter. 'She's really too big for a cot. I should get a bed.'

Wanda nodded. 'I'll watch her for you.'

Reluctantly Fleur tore herself away, suppressing pangs of envy. She couldn't manage without Wanda, but she was conscious she was missing so much of Daisy's development, from babyhood to toddler. Those years seemed to fly by so quickly, and you could never get them back.

* * *

Fleur went upstairs to Jane's flat. 'Fleur, come in, glad you could make it,' Jane greeted her. Sam, Jane's husband, came out of the kitchen. 'Fleur, great that you could come. We don't see enough of you these days.'

'Oh, I think Jane sees too much of me . . . and Daisy.'

'You haven't told her, have you?' Sam said to Jane.

'No. I thought we'd eat first.'

'Tell me what?'

Jane sat down on the sofa next to Fleur. 'Well . . . it's just that . . . we're moving.'

Fleur felt her stomach lurch. 'Moving? Where to?'

'To the country. We never intended to stay here. And . . . well . . . I'm pretty sure I'm pregnant.'

Fleur summoned up her better

feelings and and hugged her friend. 'Congratulations.'

Jane looked distressed. 'Fleur, I feel I'm letting you down . . . '

'What nonsense. I'm happy for you, and at least you're not moving far — I hope.'

'No, just nearer Mum and Dad, same village, in fact. The old rectory came on the market, bit of a ruin but lots of potential. And Sam can work a lot from home. You'll come and see us, spend lovely country weekends, you and Daisy?'

'Course, we'd love that.' Firmly Fleur pushed back her jealous pangs. What Jane had described was just the scenario she and Ben had always envisaged.

She got up and kissed Sam. 'Lucky you. You both deserve it.'

He hugged her. 'Not too sure I'm going to fit the country gent mould, and I suspect I shall miss the city buzz.'

'And I shall miss both of you, dreadfully.'

'I know,' Jane said ruefully, 'and I'll miss the flat, and you and Daisy, and the city.'

'Well, you can't change your mind now,' Sam said. 'Now come on through you two. Supper's ready.'

★ ★ ★

Over supper, Sam told Fleur about an odd occurrence outside their block of flats.

'It was quite strange,' he began, 'I came home early from work one afternoon. Jane was in the park with Alice. This guy, quite old, but a smartly dressed city type, was walking up and down past the flats and kept looking up. I was intrigued and went down to ask if I could help him, but by the time I'd got downstairs, he had gone.'

'Then, when I came back with Alice,' Jane took up the story, 'he was there again, sitting in a smart car. I was a bit nervous, thought he may be up to no good, casing the joint as they say, but then he got out of the car and asked me about the flats. Were they rented, owned, leased? Odd really, I did ask why he wanted to know, but he just said it was a government survey of foreign nationals owning property abroad. Sounded a bit fishy to me. And then . . . ' Jane hesitated.

'Then what?' Fleur said, with growing alarm.

'Then he asked me if I knew someone called Babette Remondin.'

Fleur gasped. 'But that's my mother's name!'

'I know. I didn't tell him I knew her,' Jane added hastily.

'At that point I came down,' Sam said. 'I was a bit suspicious, but he just thanked us perfectly politely, got in his car and drove off.'

'Strange,' Fleur frowned, then said, 'I wonder if it could possibly be to do with the Manoir in Brittany?'

'That's your mother's old family home isn't it?' Sam said.

'Yep. Except it's mine now, but it's a

bit of a nightmare.'

'You have tenants there, don't you?'

'Yes, but it's all in an agent's hands. I'm ashamed to say I've never been there.'

'Good Lord. Really?' Sam looked stunned. 'You've got a holiday home in Brittany and you've never even visited it?'

'It's not exactly a holiday home and it always was a bit of a mystery. Mother's family lived there for centuries, quite well off apparently, then they lost all their money and the Manoir slid into disrepair. Mum had it patched up a bit when she married Dad and rented it out, but after Dad left, she seemed to lose interest.'

'And you've never seen it? Truly?' Sam said.

'No. I've seen photos. Mum couldn't bear to go over and see it. I don't know why. I . . . well, Ben and I had plans for it, but it was quite a low priority on our list.'

'But what a legacy,' Sam said. 'Surely

though Fleur, isn't it time you paid it a visit? Even if just to check it's still there!'

'Possibly. Do you think this man who knew my mother's name could be interested in my Brittany Manoir?'

'I have no idea.' Sam poured some wine. 'But maybe this would be a good time to take a look at the place.'

'It's not our business, Sam.' Jane frowned.

'No, Jane, he's right, I've been putting it off. You see, Mum never wanted to talk about the place and I suppose I just felt, well, that I should respect her viewpoint.'

'But she did leave it to you, didn't she?' Jane said.

'She did, and it's strange, we were always short of money and she could have sold it, but she didn't. There must have been a reason for that. I guess it's time for me to find out what that reason was.' She raised her glass. 'I don't suppose you two fancy a trip to Brittany?'

Plans Are Put In Motion

Jane and Sam did fancy a trip to Brittany and after supper, Sam spent a happy hour checking planes and ferries. 'Maybe fly to Plymouth, stay with Jane's aunt in Devon, then ferry to Roscoff, Morlaix's only a short way . . . '

'Maybe I should phone the agent first,' Fleur said. 'Or can I just turn up, do you think?'

'It's your property,' Sam said. 'Surely you have a right to inspect it, check out the tenants.'

'I've left all that to the agent.'

Sam turned back to his computer. 'Hey, Jane, look, a holiday cottage near the coast, the girls would love it. See, modern kitchen, sun terrace . . . '

'Sam, don't bulldoze Fleur. Anyway,

can you take the time off work?'

'Not right now, but in a week or two. So how about it, Fleur?'

'It really is time I took a look at the Manoir, and I'd love you to come, too. I'll check my work schedule and ring Geoff Wilkins, the London agent. I'm not even sure where the French agent's office is, I'm ashamed to say.'

'Great,' Sam said. 'Then that's settled.'

Jane smiled at her husband and Fleur felt the familiar pang as Sam bent to kiss his wife.

It was still hard for her to watch couples in love, enjoying family life, planning their future. Surely that envy must fade with time.

She pushed the envy away, she had lots to be thankful for, Daisy of course, and maybe even the Manoir. But would that be a burden or a blessing?

★ ★ ★

Wanda was still up when Fleur got back to her flat. 'Daisy's sleeping like an angel,' she reported, 'now you too.'

Fleur yawned. 'I am tired.'

'I make sure I'm on time tomorrow,' Wanda said, then hesitated. 'I can ask something?'

'Sure. Go ahead.'

'My friend, Stefan, possibly tomorrow he come and talk to you. For supper? He will bring food, Polish food.'

'Well, OK, why not? I'd like to meet him again. Is he settling down in London?'

'Oh, yes. He is chef now, was teacher, now learns in London restaurant.'

'Really? That's good. But he doesn't need to bring supper.'

'He prefers. Now, you get some sleep.'

★   ★   ★

Fleur was in her office early next morning and was hard at work when Hazel arrived.

In spite of her early start, Fleur found

23

it hard to concentrate on her work of tracking down financial markets for her clients. Since yesterday, she'd had the Manoir on her mind. The Manoir de Belvoir, rarely mentioned by her mother, Babette.

All Babette's energy as a single mother was concentrated on bringing up her daughter, Fleur, seeing her through school and college and into a good career with Simkins. Finally, with her beloved Fleur happily married to Ben, she had felt able to venture out into the world again. Unfortunately, she fell slap into the arms of the smooth-talking Paul Maynard. Married in haste, Fleur's mother truly repented at leisure.

Paul Maynard was a domineering bully who made Babette's life a misery. Fleur was convinced he had driven her mother to a comparatively early grave. Fleur shuddered, vividly remembering his fearful temper when he learned Babette had left the Manoir to her daughter and not to him.

* ★ ★ ★

Fleur put in a couple of hours work, then paused to check her mobile. Two messages; one from Wanda, 'C U 2 nite — thanks'. Message two was, coincidentally, and somewhat spookily, from Geoff Wilkins, her London agent. 'Urgent, great concern re Manoir. Contact A.S.A.P.'.

She dialled his number immediately. 'Hi, Geoff, it's Fleur. Oddly enough, I was about to ring you.'

'Look, Fleur, I won't beat about the bush. It's bad news. The Manoir tenants have done a runner and I'm afraid there are rent arrears — quite a large sum.'

'But your French office . . . '

'The guy dealing with the Manoir has gone, too, obviously in cahoots with the tenants. Didn't you miss the rent from your bank account?'

'The rent was paid into a separate high interest account I haven't checked, I've been so busy lately.'

'A pity. There's damage to the place as well. Could you come in and see me?'

'Sure. I can make it this lunch-time if you're free.'

'Of course. I'll be in from midday. See you then. I'll have a list of the damages and some missing items.'

For a few moments Fleur stared unseeingly at her computer screen. It was already noon, so she switched it off and walked quickly towards Mr Simkins' office.

An hour later, she was in Geoff Wilkins' office, staring in utter dismay at the file in front of her. Geoff leaned back in his chair. 'I'm so sorry, Fleur. Would coffee help?'

Fleur smiled ruefully. 'Probably not, but it would be good. I skipped lunch.'

'Coffee coming up. Anything to eat? A sandwich?'

'No thanks. Coffee's fine.'

'I'll make it myself and give you time to digest that little lot.'

Fleur began to flip through the

papers again. 'Some of this, it's sheer vandalism. All the windows at the side, the elegant tall ones, smashed in.'

'We can fix it up again if that's what you want. I've been through the paperwork and the basic structural report doesn't seem too bad.'

'So I see. But all the furnishings and fittings have gone.'

'I don't know if you know about this,' Geoff picked up another file, 'but your mother had most of the good stuff in a store in Morlaix. The Manoir rented furnishings were quite basic.'

'Really? She never told me.'

'Perhaps sensible in the circumstances.'

At Geoff's remark, Fleur shivered as she recalled her stepfather, Paul Maynard, at her mother's funeral. He'd questioned her about some antiques, said they were his, lent to furnish the Manoir. He wanted to know if her mother had sold them, and if not, he wanted them back. Fleur had been too distressed even to think about anything like that. At that moment she had hated him. He hadn't shed a tear at the funeral and just kept asking who her mother's solicitor was.

'So,' Geoff was saying, 'what's the plan? Several options. One, sell it as it is . . .'

'Not very practical.'

'OK, option two, repair and redecorate. Find a worthy tenant, one I'd be prepared to guarantee with my life . . .'

Fleur laughed. 'Bit risky for your family! Any more options?'

'First class renovation, cost a bomb but worth it in the end. The Manoir is a very desirable property, it would fetch a good price.'

'Ideal, if I had the cash, which I haven't.' Fleur gathered up the Manoir papers. 'Let me ponder these. I've got a friend who knows a bit about building. You keep in touch with the French office, follow up with the police. I'm going over myself within the next day or so. I've fixed a week off work. I'll go back this afternoon, clear my desk, and then be off to the Manoir with Daisy.'

'The Morlaix office will take care of you and find you accommodation. The Manoir's not fit for habitation currently.'

'Fine.' Fleur held out her hand. 'No need to look so guilty, Geoff. These things happen and this could be the kick start I needed to visit the ancestral home, the Manoir de Belvoir.'

'Sounds like an adventure.'

'I do believe it could be.'

★   ★   ★

Fleur flew through her outstanding work and by late afternoon was able to pass over her files to Hazel.

'You've covered most things and I'll only need to keep an eye on a couple of files,' Hazel said.

Fleur yawned and stretched. 'There's Mr Fellowes, he usually rings a lot. Just wants a chat really, lovely widower . . . '

'For goodness' sake, Fleur, get off and enjoy your holiday. I can manage.'

'I'm actually looking forward to my trip, you know, Hazel. Something physical and practical, rather than the workings of the financial market . . . ouch, is that the time? I promised Wanda . . . '

The phone interrupted. Hazel picked it up. 'Simkins and . . . just a sec. I think she's already gone.' She covered the mouthpiece. 'For you, Fleur, do you want . . . ?'

'A client?'

'No. Personal. A Paul Maynard. Isn't he . . . ?'

'My stepfather. I haven't seen him for months. Why is he getting in touch with me now?'

'I'll tell him you've gone.'

'No, he'll only try at home. I'd better speak to him. Could you be an angel and hang on a minute, create a diversion if I signal?'

'OK.'

Fleur took the phone gingerly. 'Hello . . . er . . . Paul, I'm a bit busy and the office frowns on personal calls,' she lied.

'Oh, I'm sure they won't mind me. I'm family, Fleur, remember? It's such an age since we've seen you and it's time we got together. How's my granddaughter . . . um . . . Daisy, isn't it? We, my son, Rob, and I, would both like to see her. In fact, Robert was asking after you only the other day.'

'Was he? I hope he's well.' Fleur was polite, trying to fathom the purpose of this call. She and Paul Maynard had disliked each other from the start. She had been against her mother's disastrous second marriage and Paul had known it. The single mitigating factor of her mother's death was that she didn't ever have to see her stepfather again.

'Sorry, Paul, I am very busy.' A sixth sense warned her not to mention her proposed trip to Brittany.

'Well, can we make a date? Rob and I could call at your flat one evening, take you out to dinner.'

'Oh, no, really, I'm tied up next week . . . clients . . . I'll ring you.'

'Very well. But be sure you do. I feel

we have to make an effort, Fleur, for Babette, your mother's, sake, if nothing else.'

Fleur clenched her teeth. Paul Maynard had positively discouraged her from seeing her mother when she was alive. Babette only saw her daughter when her husband was away, preferably out of the country.

'We'll see,' she said now, and put the phone down.

★ ★ ★

On the way home, Fleur phoned and left a message for Tim Burton, her handyman/builder friend. Tim was an expert on all things practical. She had known him from schooldays and if she had a best friend, it would be Tim.

Daisy rushed to greet her as soon as she turned the key in the front door. 'Mum, Mum, Wanda, Stef, here, cooking. I'm helping.'

'Good girl.' Fleur picked up her

excited daughter and hugged her. 'Let's go and see.'

A wonderful aromatic smell wafted through the flat and into the sitting room. Wanda, cheeks flushed, came out of the kitchen to greet them. 'Fleur, Stefan is in the kitchen. I hope that is OK?'

'Of course. It smells wonderful. Just let me change and I'll be right there.'

Stefan Kotwinski, tall, dark-haired, pan in hand, came out of the kitchen. 'I hope you don't mind, Mrs Weston. I've pre-cooked most of the supper. It only needs reheating.' His English was near perfect, his broad smile warm and friendly. 'It's very good of you to let me . . . ' he started.

'Please, it's a pleasure.'

'Oh, your friend, Tim, he called. He's coming round after supper,' Wanda said. 'Stefan and I, we must leave early, but I am back early morning to see that you're in time for work.'

'Well, actually, Wanda, I'm off work tomorrow and the following week.'

'Oh, so you won't want me?'

'Well . . . sort of . . . I don't know. Let's talk over supper.'

★ ★ ★

Supper was a delicious assortment of traditional Polish dishes. There was Polish 'Hunter' stew, and the accompanying tiny dumplings entranced even the normally picky Daisy.

Wanda beamed proudly at her fiancé. 'He is good cook, yes?' she asked, as the table was cleared.

'Excellent,' Fleur agreed. 'And now, I can at least make us some coffee.'

'No, the little one is sleepy, maybe you can put her to bed. We clear, wash up, then talk.'

Once Daisy was asleep, and the kitchen had been rendered spotless, coffee and faworki, Polish sweetmeat pastry twisters, were laid out in the sitting room.

'Now,' Wanda announced, 'we tell you the news.' She looked at Stefan.

'You say, English better.'

Stefan laughed. 'Well, I did go to school in England for a few years. My father was a diplomat in London,' he explained. 'After he retired, my mother and sister went back to Poland.'

'And now you're going back, too, I guess. You and Wanda.' Fleur poured out the coffee. 'I shall miss you, Wanda, and so will Daisy.'

'No, no,' Wanda shook her head, 'not going back, stay here. Stefan works in top London restaurants. We want to stay but Daisy — Daisy starts playgroup soon, and you will have no need of me. I will need new job, references . . . '

'But Daisy isn't four yet. I still need you. Couldn't you stay on here?'

'Mrs Weston,' Stefan put in, 'Wanda and I wish to marry, have our own home, babies . . . '

'Of course you do. Stupid of me. I'm happy for you both, but I wonder, next week, Daisy and I are going away. Could you come with us, Wanda?' Briefly, Fleur explained about the Manoir.

35

Wanda was delighted. 'France, but of course! And this Manoir? Is it yours?'

'Well, yes. It's my mother's family home. I have to decide what to do with it.'

'In a bad state, you say?' Stefan frowned. 'Maybe I could come later in the week? I have many Polish friends in London, builders, plumbers, good workers.'

'It's certainly a thought, Stefan. And Wanda, you'll be a great help with Daisy.'

'I come. Very happy . . . is exciting. We go now, discuss later.' Wanda cleared the coffee cups. 'No work tomorrow?'

'Maybe an hour or so, then I need to organise my trip.'

'I will be here.'

★   ★   ★

On their way out, Wanda and Stefan met Tim Burton coming in. Fleur heard them exchange greetings.

36

'Hi, Fleur.' Tim hugged her. 'Good evening?'

'Yes. Fine. They had news.'

'And?'

'Engaged. Getting married, etcetera.'

'Oh dear. Poor Daisy. Poor you!'

'I'll survive. Tim, do you remember the Manoir I've told you about?'

'In Brittany. Yes. It was your ma's.'

'Yes. But it's mine now, and it's in trouble.' She gave him the file. 'It's all in there. I'll make fresh coffee while you look at that. I need your help, Tim.'

'Anything for you, you know that, Fleur. Ever since primary school I've been your devoted servant.' He laughed, but it was true, and since Ben died, Fleur knew she'd come to depend on Tim. He was always there when needed, even to babysit Daisy when she had to go out to see clients some evenings.

Tim had worked for his father's building company, but had left to set up on his own. Now he was branching out, hiring workers, attracting clients.

'Coffee?' he said to Fleur, as she

made no move towards the kitchen.

'Oh sure, sorry, day-dreaming. I won't be a minute and I'll look in on Daisy, too.'

He smiled. 'Say goodnight for me.'

'I will.' She crossed her fingers. If Daisy had an inkling that Tim was here, she'd be wide awake and running into the sitting room. Daisy loved Tim and Fleur knew why. Although Daisy had never known her father, there was a lot of Ben in Tim.

A Lovely Surprise

Daisy was moving restlessly with the covers off, her breathing snuffly. Fleur tucked her up and sat for a few moments waiting for her to settle, hoping she wasn't starting a cold. Tiptoeing out of the room, she went back to Tim.

Absorbed in the Manoir files, he looked up when she came in. 'Fascinating.'

'The vandalism?'

'No, the house itself, good structure but with a lot of superficial damage.'

'Can you put it right? Make it habitable?'

'I'm sure I could, but I'd have to take a look. You in a hurry?'

'I'm planning on going tomorrow.'

'Tomorrow!'

'Just to see what the situation is. I'm

taking Daisy and Wanda.'

'Did your mother ever live there herself as a child?' Tim asked.

'I think so, and then for a while after my father left. I was a baby, so I have no recollection of it. I believe there was an elderly aunt and when she died, Mother brought me to London.'

'No French relatives?'

'I don't know. I suppose there must be. Maybe I'll find out while I'm over there.'

Tim put the file to one side. 'Didn't you mention coffee about an hour ago?'

'Oh, Tim, I'm sorry. I forgot.'

'Don't worry, I can see where your thoughts are, Fleur. It's intriguing and I'd love to be involved in the restoration of the Manoir de Belvoir. In fact, I can't wait to get my hands on it. It promises to be an exciting project.'

★   ★   ★

Fleur's plans for leaving next day were thwarted by a call from Geoff Wilkins.

40

'Can you hold fire for another day, Fleur? The French agents are so upset by what's happened they're practically begging you to give them another day to clear up the worst of the mess.'

'OK, that's fair enough,' Fleur said, then, remembering her conversation with Tim, asked, 'Geoff, do you know anything about the Remondin family, my family's, history?'

'No, I don't. You could try Googling them, especially as you have a specific location in the Manoir.'

'When was it built?'

'Early nineteenth century, I think.'

'And all the stuff my mother stored? There should be some records there. Family bibles, maybe, that sort of thing.'

'Maybe. It's all in an industrial complex outside Morlaix.'

'Have you an inventory?'

'Of course. I'll e-mail you a copy.'

'Thanks, Geoff. And you know, I can't wait to get there now!'

'Delighted to hear it. I never could

fathom your complete lack of interest in the place.'

'Ah well, there you are. But rest assured, it's my number one priority now.'

What Fleur didn't tell Geoff was that, for the first time since Ben had been killed over three years ago, her mind had been momentarily free from the numbing pain of his loss.

★ ★ ★

Wanda arrived, excited, bag packed, ready for the trip. 'Thank you for last night.' She gave Daisy a hug. 'Stefan to help in France, he's putting . . . um . . . fingers out.'

'Feelers, not fingers,' Fleur grinned. 'So we'll go now, then Tim will follow. Do you think Daisy's OK? She seems a bit sniffly.'

'I think she'll be fine. We go to park now. Sunshine and fresh air will be good for her.'

'Excellent. In the meantime, I'll book

our trip. We'll hope to go tomorrow, if that's all right with you?'

'That is fine.'

As Daisy and Wanda left the flat, Fleur realised she should tell Jane about her imminent departure date just in case Sam, in his enthusiasm, was making travel arrangements himself. She waved off Daisy and Wanda and collected some brochures Sam had already popped through the letterbox on his way to work.

She ran up the stairs to Jane's flat, when a man taking the stairs down two at a time cannoned into her as she rounded the bend. 'Ooh,' she gasped, papers and brochures flying and fluttering down the stairwell.

'Gee, I am so sorry. Reckon I just didn't see you. You hurt?'

'No. Don't worry, I can . . . ' but the man was already running down the stairs to gather up the brochures and papers. As he came back towards her, Fleur saw he was tall, broad-shouldered, athletic-looking. Dark blue eyes looked quizzically at her as he handed over her papers.

'Going to France?'

His accent was American and, Fleur thought now she had a good look at him, he did look typically American in sports trousers and sweat shirt. 'Yes,' she said. 'Tomorrow, I hope. Thanks for picking these up.'

'Pleasure. The least I could do after practically knocking you downstairs.'

'Oh, I'm fine. No harm done. I wasn't looking where I was going.'

'Me neither.' They both lingered, his dark blue eyes appraising Fleur in a way she'd long forgotten was possible.

'So, France is it?' he repeated. 'And as soon as tomorrow?'

'I hope so.'

'What part?'

'Er, Brittany. Look, I should be going . . .'

'Oh, right, me too. Well . . . nice to bump into you . . .'

'Fleur.'

He put out his hand. 'Jake Merton. From the US of A, or did you guess?'

'I suppose I did,' Fleur smiled.

Neither moved, and Fleur, to her chagrin, felt herself blushing. She shook Jake Merton's hand briefly and dropped it quickly. 'I must . . . '

'Sure, me too . . . well . . . again, it was nice to bump into you, Fleur . . . maybe . . . '

But Fleur had already turned away and was running quickly up the stairs to Jane's flat.

Outside the flat, she turned back and looked down the stairwell. The American was at the bottom of the stairs in the front lobby and was looking up towards her.

He gave a tentative wave, then went out the front door.

Fleur stood outside Jane's door staring at the doorbell, waiting for her heart to stop beating. She'd run up the stairs too quickly, she reasoned.

She pushed the bell.

'Oh, Fleur, I thought it was Jake. I thought maybe he'd forgotten something. He just went down the stairs. Did you see him?' Jane said, when she opened the door.

'Yes, I did meet a man on the stairs. But I actually came to tell you that Wanda, Daisy and I are going to the Manoir tomorrow.'

'Tomorrow? Why, what's happened?'

Fleur explained why the Manoir visit was now urgent.

'I can see that,' Jane said. 'Well, maybe we can come over later. Have you time for a coffee?'

'Not really, I need to pack. And by the way, who was that man on the stairs?'

'That was Jake Merton. He was looking over the flat. We've sold it to Jake's father, who wants it for a London base. Jake happened to be over here and was just checking measurements and things. Nice guy.'

'Mmm, seems so. Look, tell Sam I'm sorry, and we'll sort out a visit soon.'

* * *

A couple of days later, as dawn was breaking, Fleur drove off the cross-Channel night ferry from Plymouth into the port of Roscoff. She had arranged to meet Geoff Wilkins' French agent here and would then be shown to the Manoir.

As soon as she got out of the car, a smartly-dressed young woman approached.

'Mrs Weston? I'm Celeste Beaumont, I recognise you from Mr Wilkins' description. And the little one in the car must be Daisy? Did you have a good trip? Calm sea?'

'Very good, thank you, and this is Wanda, who's come along to give a hand with Daisy. It's good of you to meet us so early.'

'Goodness, it's the least we could do, and I have to apologise to you for the problems with the Manoir. I feel responsible.'

Celeste's English was impeccable. 'We've worked hard these last few days,' she went on, 'and we regret so much

47

that the man who was responsible was our agent. The police are searching for him and his accomplices now. But you are here now and once at the Manoir de Belvoir, I think we have a pleasant surprise for you. You can follow my car and then perhaps breakfast: coffee, croissants . . . ?'

'We had breakfast on the ferry, thanks.'

'OK, so maybe you'll allow me to take you out to lunch while you're here?'

'That would be good, if there's time.'

'We'll make time,' Celeste said firmly.

With Daisy still asleep on Wanda's lap in the back seat, Fleur followed Celeste's car through the dawn-quiet roads of Brittany towards Morlaix. As they drove through the ancient town with its wonderful overarching viaduct, her excitement grew. She'd practically almost forgotten she was half French, and now she was in the land of her ancestors. She tried to relax and concentrate on keeping her guide's car in sight, but her hands on the steering wheel were tense.

Daisy stirred. 'Where's this?'

'France, Daisy, love, where your granny used to live.'

'Not Dora granny?'

'Not Dora gran, she's in Scotland.'

Now they were leaving the town and approaching gently sloping green fields. Fleur almost missed the sharp right turn Celeste was signalling. She led them up a long winding drive, trees and shrubs on either side. Spring sunshine was breaking through the misty dawn as Celeste stopped her car in front of a three storeyed dwelling, stone built, with three symmetrical rows of tall, shuttered windows. There was a small building close by, with a bell tower and cross, possibly the family chapel. Fleur took a deep breath and stepped out of the car. Wanda followed, carrying a sleepy Daisy.

Celeste looked at Fleur anxiously. 'There is much work to do, but it is a lovely house, yes?'

'Yes, yes, it is.' Fleur went up a broad flight of stone steps onto the terrace. The slabs were cracked and broken but on a sunny day ... with tables and chairs?

Celeste pointed out some skips by the side of the house which were piled high with junk of every sort: tin drums, broken chairs, planks and a mountain of empty bottles. 'Men are coming today to replace the windows and mend the shutters. And the chapel has been used as a storeroom, but if you want it restored ... '

'We'll see, Celeste. But the house is lovely. I thought — well, I imagined it as some sort of ruin.'

'Oh, no. The Manoir is a beautiful building. You'll see, we'll bring it back to life.'

'Can we go inside?' Fleur asked.

'Only a little today, some of the floors ... '

Fleur picked up Daisy and gingerly they pushed open the double front door and entered the Manoir.

A large entrance hall led to spacious rooms, more broken windows, graffiti on the walls, cobwebs, dirt and dust, but out of the glassless windows there were wonderful views of sweeping parkland.

'So much land. I never imagined . . . ' Fleur stood, entranced, as Daisy sucked her thumb. Wanda was wide-eyed.

'And so close to the town, you can walk there in ten minutes,' Celeste said.

'Hungry, Mummee.' Daisy struggled to be put down.

'Just a sec, love. Celeste, do we have any accommodation booked? Geoff said . . . '

'Ah. Now here is the surprise I promised you. We do have a cottage here in the grounds.'

'Part of the Manoir?'

'Yes, and it's undamaged. Shall I show you?'

'Please. That would be lovely.'

Celeste went ahead, stepping through the dewy grass towards a small, rustic-looking building. A flight of stone steps led to a substantial wooden door.

'Here you are, a small barn conversion: sitting room, two bedrooms, kitchen off the sitting room, all modern conveniences. Modernised a few years ago before the horror tenants arrived. A single guy took it, looked after it really well, but left a few months ago. He couldn't stand his neighbours.'

'It's lovely. I never realised,' Fleur said.

Celeste looked curious. 'Did you really not know? Surely Geoff Wilkins . . . '

'Oh, I'm sure he did, but . . . I . . . that was probably when . . . around the time my husband, Ben, was killed.'

Celeste looked stricken. 'Oh, I'm sorry. So sorry.'

'Please, don't be. I suppose I just hid away from everything and concentrated on Daisy. I was seven months' pregnant when the accident . . . '

'Oh, oh dear.'

'Please, don't worry. Daisy, Wanda,

what do you think? We're going to stay here!'

'Dolly house,' Daisy clapped in approval. 'Dinky dolly house. We can live here, Mum?'

'Well, for a few days anyway.'

Celeste gave her the keys. 'The men are coming to work on the main house today, so if there's anything you need, Mrs . . . ?'

'Fleur, please! And thank you so much, Celeste. I feel as though I've come home. Isn't that odd?'

'I'm glad you feel like that. We're hoping we'll be allowed to carry on working for you for a long time. The Manoir has got letting and holiday home potential. It just needs some love and attention, something it hasn't had for a very long time, I think . . . ' Her mobile rang. 'Excuse me, it's the office.'

Celeste answered her phone. 'Oh, I see. Yes, she's here beside me. OK, switch it through.' She handed the mobile to Fleur. 'For you.'

'Who . . . ? Maybe Tim, he promised

to phone. Hi, Fleur Weston here.'

'Hello, Fleur, my dear, it's Paul. I'm so pleased to have caught you. Rob and I have just arrived, we're in Roscoff and we'll be with you very shortly. Rather naughty of you to run off without telling us, but never mind, we'll see you very soon. We know where the Manoir is.'

'But I don't . . . ' The connection broke. 'Blast, blast, blast! How on earth did he know?'

'Bad news?' Celeste asked.

'Very bad news. Couldn't be worse.'

A Nasty Encounter For Fleur

'Fleur, what is it?' Celeste instinctively moved towards her. 'You look alarmed, frightened . . . '

'Not frightened, just furious. And maybe apprehensive. Whenever he turns up it's usually trouble.'

'But who is he, this man who is at our office?'

'Paul Maynard, my late mother's husband. Why did he follow me here? How could he even know I was here?'

'There is a problem?'

Fleur's laugh was bitter. 'There usually is a problem when my stepfather is involved. He made my mother's final years an absolute misery.'

Wanda picked up Daisy, who had started to toddle towards the house. 'No, Daisy, not on your own. Fleur, I did not know about your stepfather. He is trouble?'

'Usually, and there's no love lost between us.'

'Can I help?' Celeste offered. 'Maybe phone the office?'

'No, it's too late, and anyway, that wouldn't stop him. Besides, I don't want to involve you in whatever game he's playing.'

'But I am involved. You are my client, my responsibility, while you are here. I will stay, of course, to see what he wants. If he has left the office, he'll be here soon.'

'I'd be very grateful for your support, Celeste.'

Fleur turned to Wanda. 'Wanda, I don't want Daisy here when he comes, could you take her into town? It's not far.'

'Of course, that would be fun for Daisy — a French town!' Wanda put Daisy down as Fleur knelt to speak to her. 'Daisy, love, how would you like Wanda to take you into town, have lunch at a creperie.'

'What is that?'

'It's where you can eat delicious pancakes, sweetie, with syrup. Or savoury with cheese. Crepes are special to Brittany, which is where we are now. Your daddy and I loved them and you will too, I'm sure. I'll see you later at the little house in the garden.'

'At dinky dolly house, yes.' Daisy clapped her hands then took a firm hold of Wanda's hand. 'To capery, please.'

'Let's go then,' Wanda said.

'Thanks very much, you're a real help.' Fleur was relieved. Whatever Paul Maynard was up to, she didn't want Daisy to be anywhere near him.

'Perhaps we shop a little, too,' Wanda said, as she buttoned up Daisy's coat, 'and if the little one is not too tired, we can explore the town a little.'

'Thank you, Wanda. What would I do without you?'

'No need to think of that yet. I am here a while.'

'If you want take the car, just leave our bags somewhere.'

'The chapel is open,' Celeste said, 'you can leave them there. The workmen will arrive soon and they'll keep an eye on your luggage.'

'OK, see you later,' Fleur said, and kissed Daisy. 'Be a good girl for Wanda.'

★ ★ ★

'Wanda is a relative?' Celeste asked.

'No, she's Daisy's nanny. I work full-time, you see. She's like family but she's getting married soon. Her fiancé, Stefan, is from Poland, too.'

'I see. But it must be hard work for you with a job and children.'

'Child. I don't have any other family.'

'Ah! I didn't know. I'm so . . . '

'Don't, please, be sorry. I'm very lucky. I have a good job, good friends, and now I have the Manoir to think about.'

'But . . . ' Celeste floundered, 'no aunts, sister, brothers . . . ?'

'Not a one.' Fleur had to laugh at Celeste's horrified expression. 'I take it you have a large family.'

'Indeed.' Celeste rolled her eyes. 'Like an octopus . . . claws everywhere, and all in this area.'

'I think the word is tentacles, but you're very lucky,' Fleur grinned.

* * *

As Fleur and Celeste neared the Manoir, Fleur stopped abruptly. 'He's here already,' she said tersely.

A sleek, expensive-looking black car was parked outside the Manoir and two men were standing looking up at the building, their backs to Fleur and Celeste.

'Good grief. Both of them. Rob, too,' Fleur said.

'Rob?'

'His son, not such a bad lot as his father, but completely dominated by him.'

Both men turned round, one white-haired, one fair. The older man, Paul

Maynard, wore an expensive dark suit and what looked like a cashmere coat. Thick set and powerful, the smile on his face didn't reach his eyes.

'What are you doing here?' Fleur asked coolly when she reached the car.

Rob Maynard, more casually dressed than his father, greeted Fleur. 'Hi, Fleur, long time since I've seen you.'

Paul Maynard ignored his son as he said to Fleur, 'Come, come, Fleur, not a very warm welcome. You can do better than that, especially since we're here to help you. A bad business this,' he gestured towards the Manoir, 'you've let the property go to rack and ruin. You obviously need my input.'

'I most certainly do not! And what's more . . . '

'I'd no idea it was in such a terrible state, and rent arrears and debts on the property, too.' Paul cut across what Fleur was saying.

'Where did you hear that?' Celeste asked sharply.

Paul turned his attention to her. 'And you are?'

'Mrs Weston's agent from the French office of Wilkins, London.'

'Ah, so you're part of this.' He pointed to the Manoir. 'We can probably sue your firm for incompetent management.'

'It's none of your business,' Fleur put in hotly, before Celeste could respond.

'It is very much my business,' Paul countered. 'I have an interest in my late wife's property and a good thing I do, seeing the state it's in. You, Fleur, are obviously not capable of looking after the estate properly. You must . . . '

'Dad,' Rob interrupted, 'Fleur is . . . '

'Quiet, Rob, I'm dealing with this. I'll do the talking, you just concentrate on the paperwork and take note of any slanderous accusations Fleur might, unwittingly, of course . . . '

'Stop it!' Fleur raised her voice while Celeste put out a restraining hand.

'Mr Maynard, could you explain? You surely can't make a claim on the estate.

It belongs solely to Mrs Weston. I admit we've made errors in administration, but we're dealing with them. I can't see what your interest is.'

'I'm sure you can't, but your office must have been pocketing a hefty management fee since my wife's death and doing nothing to earn it. We will be looking for compensation.'

'Just go away,' Fleur snapped. 'You've no business here.'

Paul Maynard turned to Rob and snapped his fingers. 'Paper, Rob, the file. Come on, don't just stand there.'

'We do have evidence,' Rob started to say, as he passed a folder to his father.

'That's enough, Rob, you don't need to explain, the papers speak for themselves.' Paul Maynard thrust the folder at Fleur. 'Read, and you will see I have a perfectly legitimate claim to a share of my wife's property, Manoir de Belvoir, and its surrounding acres.'

'Impossible.'

'Not so, my dear Fleur. For a start, you were not the least interested in the legal niceties of your mother's will. Perhaps you should have been. It was, after all, which was not surprising, a very sloppy document.'

'Don't you dare say anything against my mother! You made her life a misery, she would never have left a single stone of her family home to you!'

'Examine the papers, the legal case presented by my lawyer, the plans your mother and I had for developing this place . . .'

Fleur held her hand up.

'Just stop, now. And I suggest you leave my property immediately.'

'Oh no, I don't think so. I'm not leaving Brittany for a while. You're out of your depth, Fleur, massive expenditure is needed to repair the Manoir and you can't possibly afford it.'

'OK, Dad, I think Fleur's got the message. Let her look at the papers.'

Paul Maynard ignored his son. 'I'm not totally unsympathetic, Fleur, and I am prepared to help you in spite of your attitude. I'll make you a generous offer for the Manoir, enough for a little coastal property down south, a holiday home for you and Daisy.'

Celeste stepped forward. 'Mr Maynard, I think you should leave now, men are due shortly to carry out work on the Manoir. I'll contact Geoff Wilkins in London, consult our lawyers . . . '

'No,' Fleur started, but Celeste put a restraining hand on her arm. 'Mr Maynard, if you would leave me your contact details . . . '

'I'd prefer to stay for a while. We haven't completed our survey of the property.'

As he spoke, a couple of heavy lorries rumbled up the drive. Celeste waved to the first driver. 'My uncle, Jean Pierre, boss of the property firm working on the Manoir. It's best if you leave, he won't be pleased to be hindered.'

The first lorry stopped and a huge burly man jumped down from the cab and enveloped Celeste in a bear hug and kissed her on both cheeks. As they spoke rapid French, the driver's smile turned to a frown as he looked across to where Paul and Rob Maynard were standing. At a snap of his fingers several men jumped from the two lorries to form a protective barrier around the two women.

Celeste said, 'Best leave now, Mr Maynard.'

'Come on, Dad,' Rob said. 'Sorry, Fleur, I'm sure we can work something out.' He turned back to his father. 'Dad, you've done what you came to do; it's a shock to Fleur and you can't blame her.'

'You stupid fool, of course I blame her. Her and that stupid woman, her mother. She was . . .'

'Dad, it doesn't help. Come on.' Firmly, Rob bundled his father into the passenger seat of their car, then drove away, neatly avoiding the randomly parked lorries.

Celeste said to Fleur, 'Give me a minute to have a word with Jean Pierre, to check out his plans for today's workload, then we'll walk back to La

Maison du Jardinier, your little cottage. I've put provisions in there. I hoped you'd be staying.'

'Thanks, Celeste.' Fleur looked anxious. 'Can he really do any of those things he said? I mean, the Manoir's mine, unconditional, isn't it?'

'Let's just look at the papers he brought.'

*　*　*

In the comparative peace and calm of the little cottage, Fleur leafed through the documents in the file while Celeste made coffee. It was warm and cosy, the coffee's fragrance calming.

'Anything yet?' Celeste put the cafétier on the table, along with a plate of biscuits. 'Better eat these, my aunt made them especially to welcome you.'

'Your aunt?'

'Mmm. Tante Louise, she has a small café in the town and Uncle Jacques runs the bakery. Best in Brittany.'

'How many aunts and . . . ?'

'Countless. Also nephews and nieces. You must meet them, they are all so interested in the future of the Manoir. Its first owner was a philanthropist, very popular, he financed many worthwhile projects in the area.'

'It must be great to be part of such a large family,' Fleur said.

'We have our ups and downs, but it's mainly ups. Are you feeling better now? The meeting with your stepfather was not very nice.'

'They never are,' Fleur said, flicking through the documents. 'There's a letter here from a French lawyer who's advising my stepfather to contest Mother's will. Surely that's too late now, it's nearly two years, and here . . .' she pulled out a folded sheet of paper, 'some sort of plan, notes on a conversion and . . . oh no, Celeste, my mother's signature as well as his. But Mother would never have agreed to this.'

'We'll have our lawyers look it over. Is there anything else?'

'A letter signed Babette Maynard agreeing to Paul's plans for converting the Manoir into apartments. But she'd never have agreed to that, I know she wouldn't. Mother always wanted to retain the true character of the Manoir. And the letter's computer generated. Mother never had anything to do with computers.'

'Someone else could have drawn up the documents, you mean,' Celeste said.

'And the date on the plans is when she was so ill. Just weeks before she died.'

Celeste poured more coffee. 'I wonder . . . so far it looks questionable, more as if Monsieur Maynard is trying to scare you off. He didn't know you were coming here, did he?'

'Not that I know of. It was Geoff Wilkins who contacted me because the tenants had gone.'

'I'll try to find out if we have a, how do you call it, a skunk in the office?'

Fleur had to laugh. 'A mole I think

you mean, though skunk would equally apply.'

'Also, we need to get legal advice. French property laws are different from English, as are inheritance laws.'

'But Mother lived in England most of her life.'

'But she was born French?'

'Of course. I always thought of her as British. Daft, really, because she was French.'

'Naturalised?'

'I'm ashamed to say I don't know. Mother never talked about the past.'

'And your father?'

'She never once spoke of him. I can't believe it now, but I never asked.'

'You don't know where he lives?'

'No idea. He cut us completely adrift before I was born. But one thing I am certain of is that Mother had too great a regard for her ancestral past to let Paul Maynard have any say in the Manoir's future. It's mine. Paul can do whatever he likes but I'm going ahead with my plans.'

'Which are?' Celeste sipped her coffee.

Fleur took a breath, suddenly her path was crystal clear. Whatever it took, she knew now exactly what her intentions were. 'I am the Manoir's owner, I shall restore it and what's more . . . ' she could hardly believe her next words, they were instinctive, without rational thought, but she knew with certain and sure clarity it was what she wanted, 'I'm staying here and I'm going to live in the Manoir de Belvoir, whatever it takes.'

Celeste hugged her. 'Bravo, Fleur. And you won't be on your own. I'll help all I can and you will have the support of the entire Dubois family. I'll see to that.'

Fleur Meets Jake Merton Again

Fleur was determined to steam ahead with the renovation of the Manoir. 'I don't have a clear idea as to what I want right now,' she told Celeste, 'but I don't want a patch-up job. I want permanency. This is going to be my home, mine and Daisy's.'

'Permanency? But your job in London . . . ?'

'I'll think about that later. Right now, I want to restore the Manoir to whatever was its brightest and best period. I'll commute, I'll work from home, whether that's the Manoir or London and . . . ' She stopped, alight with enthusiasm. 'I'll resign from Simkins!'

'Fleur, don't you think maybe it would be a good idea to see just how much this will cost and how you would live in this house? It is lovely, but isn't it a bit large for you and Daisy on your own?'

'Easy,' Fleur said, 'the Manoir will be a hotel, four star at least.'

Celeste put her hand on Fleur's arm. 'Fleur, my dear client, I have to tell you that unless you have won the lottery or inherited a fortune, you will never succeed with this venture. Have you any idea how much it would cost?'

'Oh Celeste, think positive. Lots of people leave their jobs to run hotels, bars and restaurants. All right, I've no experience in the trade, but I'm a fast learner and I know about business. OK,' she compromised at the sight of Celeste's horrified expression, 'I'll start with bed and breakfast. Look how close we are to Roscoff, the channel port. It's a perfect tourist stop-over, and once they stop, they'll want to stay here. The Manoir will be so lovely they won't want to leave.'

'Shouldn't you at least speak to my

uncle Jean Pierre before you get carried away?'

'Of course, of course.' Fleur tried to speak more soberly but excitement swirled around her brain and, for the first time since Ben's death, she felt properly alive, full of enthusiasm and looking forward to the future.

* * *

When Wanda and Daisy came back from town, Daisy came running up to greet her mother. 'Mum, Mum, I had crepes and frits!' She flung herself into Fleur's arms.

'Oh dear, chips and pancakes . . . that's not very healthy, Daisy.'

'I'm sorry, Fleur,' Wanda said, 'I just couldn't say no to her.'

'Oh never mind, we're on holiday.' Fleur swung Daisy around. 'How would you like to live here, in Brittany, in the Manoir?'

'In dolly house?'

'Well, at first maybe.' Fleur tried to

bring herself down to earth. 'OK, Wanda, perhaps you'd settle Daisy for a nap in the cottage. And, Wanda, how long can you stay here? I do so need your help.'

'As long as you wish. Stefan has a few day's holiday and, would you believe, he has never been to France.'

'Great. He'll be very welcome.

'Now, Celeste, let me talk to Jean Pierre, then we'll go back to your office to see how the legal land lies. Paul Maynard won't push me out of my home, the Manoir de Belvoir.' She just loved saying its name out loud.

★ ★ ★

For the next hour, Fleur was a woman with a mission. Jean Pierre had little English, so with Celeste as translator, she did a tour of the Manoir, making copious notes, her brain whirling with plans, sensible and not so sensible.

To Fleur's delight, Jean Pierre pronounced many of the Manoir's rooms as *pas mal*, not bad, and said that repairs would be possible. To Fleur's final question, 'How much would it take to restore the Manoir?' he scrawled a figure on his note-pad and presented it to her.

The sum of euros had a lot of zeroes and Fleur frowned as she passed it to Celeste. 'I know he's your uncle, but you know more about this than I do. Is that a fair estimate? It looks like an enormous amount to me.'

Celeste scanned the list and turned to her uncle with a stream of rapid French which was incomprehensible to Fleur. Then Celeste crossed out Jean Pierre's figure and scribbled another which she showed to Fleur.

'That's much less,' Fleur gasped. 'I don't want to do him down . . . '

'No, no, it's normal practice. Uncle Jean would have been amazed if you'd accepted the first estimate.'

'I'm so grateful, Celeste. So what about the time scale?'

There was another rapid exchange of

French before Celeste said, 'He'll give it priority, but it depends on whether he can recruit more workers.'

'I think I may be able to help there. I have a good friend in England who could maybe bring a few English builders over.'

Celeste turned again to Jean Pierre, who spoke to his foreman who'd been with them on the inspection tour. Both men laughed and nodded and Jean Pierre put out his hand to Fleur.

'It's a deal,' Celeste translated.

Fleur shook hands with a now beaming Jean Pierre who kissed her on both cheeks before plunging back into the Manoir with his foreman.

Fleur turned excitedly to Celeste. 'You see? It's all going to work out. I'm going to have bed and breakfast to start, maybe add a restaurant or bistro . . .'

Celeste looked sceptical. 'Have you any experience at all?'

'No, but I might just know someone who does have experience. Oh, it's all so exciting, Celeste, don't you think?'

'I do but . . . ' She hesitated. 'There's so much work to do. I am behind you, but just promise me you'll think hard about it all.'

'I shall, I promise, but I do need another life. I need to be with Daisy, too, I hardly see her in my present job. If I can work in the Manoir, it'd be ideal.'

'What about your stepfather? He strikes me as a determined man.'

'Another reason for my decision. I know my mother wouldn't want him to have anything whatever to do with Manoir de Belvoir. And everything will be much easier with your help.'

'You can count on it, and all the Dubois family too. Uncle Jean Pierre is quite bowled over already.'

'Really? That's good news.'

'And as for Daisy, at the moment in our family there isn't a child of Daisy's age. Daisy will be, what do you say, spoiled rotten? You'll have no worry about child care here.'

Impulsively Fleur hugged her new friend. 'I can't wait to start,' she said.

★ ★ ★

The next few days flew by. Jean Pierre, as promised, gave the Manoir top priority. Skip after skip lumbered down the winding drive, and after three days, he was ready to start on the task of restoration. Celeste had the firm's lawyer looking into Paul Maynard's claim to the Manoir and he promised a verdict shortly, but did say his case looked full of holes.

After a phone call from Fleur, Tim was due to arrive at the Manoir the following day, with a promise of workers from his father's business.

Wanda was due to leave at the end of the week to report back to Stefan and was hopeful she would be returning to Brittany with him. She was as excited as Fleur about the prospects for the Manoir, and thought Stefan, as a trained chef, would be very interested in Fleur's restaurant idea.

As for Daisy, she was received with open arms by the aunts, mums and grannies of the Dubois family and, ironically, Fleur now saw less of her than she did in England. But Daisy was always happy to return at the end of the day to the dinky dolly house. And already she had a smattering of French.

*   *   *

A week later, Fleur and Daisy met Tim from the ferry at Roscoff. 'Goodness, you look well, Fleur.' Tim kissed her on the cheek. 'And you,' he picked up Daisy, 'must have grown two inches at least.'

'Bonju,' Daisy giggled, ''allo Tim.'

'Wow, a native speaker. So, tell me all about it, Fleur.'

'I told you on the phone — most of it. You need to see the Manoir now. I can't wait to show you.'

'I've got a good idea already from the pictures you sent me. And I've a queue of blokes lined up to come over and start work.'

'Really? I hope they get on with Jean Pierre. You know what the English and French can be like when they're together.'

By now they were in the car driving to the Manoir. 'You do know what you're doing?' Tim said. 'It's a terrific undertaking. And what about your job?'

'I've spoken to Mr Simkins and I'm going over in a day or so. I'll maybe get a bit of part-time work at home. And I'll probably put the flat on the market.'

'Sell the flat! That'll be burning your boats. Shouldn't you wait a bit?'

'Why? I want to do this Tim, and I'll need the money I can get for the flat. I'll have to take out a big enough loan as it is.'

'Didn't you say Paul, your step-father, is causing trouble?'

'Celeste's office is handling it. They think his claim is spurious. French laws about inheriting property are very strict and they don't think Paul Maynard has much of a chance. I'll fight him to the end, anyway.'

As they turned into the Manoir's drive, Tim exclaimed, 'Hey, is this it? Lovely grounds, more like a park.'

'See, see,' Daisy bounced up and down in the back. 'Over there! Dinky dolly house where we live.'

★ ★ ★

Spring was taking hold, showing the Manoir at its best, as they drew up to the front of the building. A team of gardeners had already mown, pruned and raked gravel paths and planted beds with spring flowers. Sunlight glinted from replacement windows; a workman on a ladder was repairing and replacing damaged shutters.

'I don't believe this,' Tim gasped, 'you said it was practically derelict, Fleur.'

'It was, and inside there's still loads to do, but we thought if we did the front first, we could put the picture on the brochure.'

'Brochure!' Tim squawked. 'What brochure?'

'The bed and breakfast brochure. I might as well try to catch some passing trade this summer.'

'Trade? Bed and breakfast? What are you talking about, Fleur?'

'Oh come on, Tim, the house is far too big for Daisy and me on our own. And I have to make it pay.'

'But, Fleur, you're an accountant, not a . . .'

'Shush, Tim. Now come on inside to meet Jean Pierre and his team, then we'll go to our cottage. There's a tiny spare room which I hope will be OK for you. Oh, and I'd like you to come with me tomorrow to look over Mum's furniture in store in Morlaix. You've an eye for antiques and quality stuff. You'll know what I could maybe sell to raise some cash.'

★ ★ ★

Tim took Daisy's hand as they walked up the terrace steps to the house. 'You're different, Fleur,' he remarked.

'How am I different?'

Tim hesitated. 'You're more alive. Focussed. Excited.'

'I am excited, Tim.'

Jean Pierre, beaming broadly, came out to meet them.

'Bonjour. C'est Tim?'

Fleur nodded. 'And fortunately, he speaks French, so I'm leaving you two to it.'

★ ★ ★

An hour later, his head spinning, Tim walked across the parkland to the cottage, La Maison du Jardinier. Daisy was playing with a couple of older children in the garden.

'Coming for breakfast?' Tim called.

'Had it. I'm playing now.' Daisy tossed a ball to one of the girls.

'OK, see you later then.'

Fleur came out of the house bringing

out a laden tray. 'Don't go too far away, Daisy, we're going to the market with Tim soon.'

'OK.'

Tim followed Fleur up the stone steps into a small sitting room. 'Dinky is about right,' he laughed.

'It suits us; lovely modern kitchen, huge garden for Daisy, all sixteen acres of it, but we'll move into the main house as soon as it's habitable and rent this out to tourists. Do you think you'll be able to work with Jean Pierre?'

'Easy, he's a great guy. No problem.'

Fleur poured out coffee. 'Croissants and honey, pain au chocolat; very French!'

An hour later, Fleur, Tim and Daisy left the Manoir to walk into town. Although it was Saturday morning, Jean Pierre and most of his team were working on the house. 'Unheard of, apparently,' Fleur said as they walked past. 'Usually Saturday is a family day, but Jean Pierre wants to press ahead, lucky for me. Oh, and, he's invited us to a Sunday Spring barbecue at his house on the coast to meet the Dubois family.'

'Dubois?'

'Celeste, Wilkins' agent, Jean Pierre's niece. She's a fantastic help. I am lucky, I couldn't do this without her.'

'I look forward to meeting her.'

By now they were near the town, the streets already crowded with market shoppers, queueing, browsing, gossiping or bargaining with the stall holders.

'Hold on to my hand, Daisy,' Fleur said. 'I don't want to lose you in this crowd.'

Tim was eyeing the tasty cooked meats set out on the food stalls.

Fleur laughed. 'You look like a kid at Christmas. I'll buy you a slice of pork for lunch.'

'Would you really? I'd like that.' Tim kissed her on the cheek, then turned his head and frowned. 'Hey, do you know that guy, Fleur? He's staring at you as though he knows you. Over there, by that cheese stall.'

'Where? I can't . . . ' then Fleur's

stomach felt as though it had physically turned over, her heart hammered and her cheeks flushed. 'Oh,' was all she could say.

'So you do know him. He's coming over.'

Fleur instinctively put her arm through Tim's.

'Hello there, what a coincidence. It is you, isn't it? The girl on the stairs in London? Fleur? Jane's block of flats. How extraordinary.' Dark blond hair, deep sapphire blue eyes, broad, tall and tanned. It was the American.

'Jake, wasn't it?' Fleur managed faintly.

His eyes held hers and he nodded. The market bustle seemed to fade as their eyes stayed locked together.

'Jake?'

'Fleur?'

Simultaneously, two outside voices broke the silence.

'Oh, sorry.' Jake turned to the woman by his side. 'This is Amanda. Amanda, this is Fleur Weston from London.' To

Tim he said, 'Jake Merton,' and held out his hand.

'Tim Hughes. You and Fleur know each other, then?'

'Not exactly, we met very briefly in London.'

How did he know her name? Fleur thought. Had she told him?

'Such a crush, we'd better move on, Jake.' The Amanda woman spoke sharply. 'And we're short of time.'

'Oh, we'll be fine.' Jake looked down at Daisy, who was clinging to Fleur's hand. 'Hello, what's your name?'

'Daisy Weston, what's yours?'

'Jake Merton, and I'm pleased to meet you, Daisy.'

'Look, why don't we all go for coffee and an ice cream for Daisy? This is such a coincidence and I can hardly believe . . . '

'Sorry,' Tim interrupted and looked at his watch. 'We've a lot to do. Maybe another time.'

'Oh,' Fleur said, 'but we could . . . ' Her eyes were on Jake.

Amanda tugged at Jake's arm. 'Yes,

maybe another time. Come on, Jake, your father's going to call from the States so we must get back to the hotel.'

Tim took Fleur's arm. 'We must move on, too, Fleur. That pork, it's selling fast. And you did promise.'

'All right.' But as Fleur was pulled away, she turned to look over her shoulder at Jake Merton. He was doing exactly the same thing, looking intently back at her.

'Friend of yours?' Tim asked.

'No, it's what he said, we met on the stairs going up to Jane's and Sam's flat. I was going up, he was coming down, I dropped some papers, he picked them up. That was all.'

'Really? From the looks of the two of you it seemed as if it was much more than that. Did you want to have coffee with them? I didn't mean to rush you off.'

'I don't think so. Anyway, his wife didn't seem to be keen.'

Another Strange Coincidence

Tim's next task was to return to England and recruit some of his father's builders. Wanda planned an exploration of the local beaches with Daisy, leaving Fleur to drive Tim to the ferry at Roscoff. On the way, they called at the storage unit in Morlaix where her mother's furniture was kept.

Monsieur Dupre, manager of the repository, greeted Fleur. 'I am so pleased to meet you. Madame Remondin spoke of you, Fleur isn't it? And this gentleman, he is your husband?'

'No. Tim Hughes, a friend who will advise me on what to keep at the Manoir to recreate something of its former style.'

'Of course. And you are going to live there with your family?'

'Yes. I have a small daughter, and I need to run the Manoir as a bed and breakfast business. I'm a widow, you see.'

'Oh dear, I am so sorry. I didn't know. Forgive me. But the gentleman who came here last week didn't mention you. He had his son with him.'

'And who was that?' Fleur said sharply, though she knew with a sinking heart that there was only one person it could be.

'Monsieur Maynard, Madame Remondin's husband. He came to collect some pieces, view some paintings. He has a large collection I believe.'

'But Mr Maynard has no claim to anything here. He shouldn't be taking anything!' Fleur said in alarm.

'Oh dear. But he had receipts for the articles he took. Only last week he had the pieces collected, I dealt with him myself, he said he had a house in France. You see here, the paperwork is all in order.'

Fleur quickly scanned the list; dining

table, Chippendale chairs, early nineteenth century cabinets, escritoires, chaise longues, lamps, pictures, artefacts, sets of china, cutlery.

'Quite a van load.' Monsieur Dupre looked mortified. 'But as you see, he had proof of ownership. I assumed Monsieur Maynard . . . '

'Please don't worry, Mr Dupre,' Fleur interrupted, 'it's all my fault. My mother never encouraged me to take an interest in the Manoir. That's no excuse, of course, but I'm determined to make amends now for my past neglect.'

'Of course, of course, and I shall not release anything in future without contacting you first. You're at the Manoir, I assume?'

'Yes.'

'And you are really going to run it as a what do you call it, a bed and breakfast?'

'Yes, it's the only way I can keep it in the family.' As she heard her own words Fleur felt a strange thrill . . . *in the family . . . her* family.

'Well, I wish you the best of luck,' Monsieur Dupre was saying.

'Thank you, that's kind. Tim, have you finished here?'

'No, but I'll come back, if that's all right, Monsieur Dupre?'

'Of course. I will be sure to make myself available.'

* * *

Next morning, Wanda left for London to report back to Stefan, who had already recruited a Polish plumber and two electricians. He was excited about Fleur's plan for a bistro and constantly e-mailed her with ideas, plans and even recipes. The marriage was temporarily put on hold. As Wanda explained to Fleur, 'a wedding we can do any time, a bistro in France is only once.'

Fleur herself was on site through all the daylight hours, choosing fabrics, china and planning an advertising campaign. She loved the bustle, the problem solving, the constant activity. She regretted losing time with Daisy but her daughter was more than happy to be brought into the Dubois clan. They had become her family and she was in danger of being spoilt with love and attention. Fleur made it a rule to spend an hour or two with her in the ever-lengthening spring evenings.

With so much going on, she found it impossible to leave Brittany. She phoned Mr Simkins and was told the firm were agreeable to an extended leave of absence with her old job back if she ever wanted it.

Celeste was dealing with the planning regulations, and the whole raft of E.U. requirements for health and safety.

Tim returned with his builders and at first there was some friction between the differing nationalities but everyone soon settled down. Tim and Celeste spent a lot of time together checking building rules and regulations.

Then one mid-May morning, Jean Pierre made an announcement to Fleur and the gang of workers: 'Manoir de Belvoir will be open by mid-June. Fleur, start your advertising campaign right now. Meantime, the Dubois barbecue is next Sunday and all are invited.'

★ ★ ★

Fleur wrote to her stepfather telling him of her intentions to turn the Manoir into a thriving bed and breakfast with accompanying bistro. He replied, threatening a court action.

'Bluff and bluster,' Celeste said. 'Ignore him, put your mind to those elegant furnishings and fittings for the Manoir de Belvoir's grand opening. You've done a wonderful job and the bistro's almost ready isn't it?'

'Yep, weekends at first, just to see how it goes.'

'And your friend, Tim, works very hard. He is a very charming man, I think.'

At Celeste's words, Fleur recalled

that she hadn't seen much of Tim lately. She'd assumed it was work that had kept him in Celeste's office for many hours. She pushed away the unworthy pang of regret for the passing of Tim's previous single-minded devotion.

'Yes, a very charming man, Celeste,' she agreed.

★ ★ ★

Jean Pierre's home near the coast turned out to be a small chateau with a swimming pool. The barbecue was an established annual event with all his family and friends invited. It was an all-day affair, starting with a champagne breakfast after early morning church. An afternoon of organised games and swimming races was followed by a short siesta and the evening barbecue, where more guests from the village swelled the numbers.

Wanda and Fleur were in the pool with Daisy. 'She is like small fish,' Wanda gasped as she touched the side of the pool seconds after Daisy. 'Race again,' she challenged Daisy, 'you too, Fleur, maybe she beat you too.'

'Not me. I'm done. You two carry on. It's just a pity poor Stefan's stuck in the kitchen.'

'He loves it in there,' Wanda said. Then, 'Hey, Daisy, come back! Don't cheat! Fleur, give us the start.'

'Right. You ready? Ready, steady . . . '

'Go,' said a masculine voice as Daisy and Wanda struck out together. Fleur turned around in the pool, shielded her eyes against the glare of the sun and saw the tall figure of Jake Merton smiling down on her.

'Hi, what a coincidence. Again.' He put out his hand to help her from the pool. His grip was strong and she felt as light as a feather as she was lifted out to join him at the poolside. 'Thanks.'

'I won! I won!' Daisy shouted.

'She sure did.' Wanda shook her head. 'I can't keep up with Little Miss Mermaid here.'

'You're going to be a great swimmer,

Daisy,' Fleur said proudly.

'I am, I am. Can we have a pool, Mum, at the Manoir?'

'Perhaps, one day. Come on in now and get dressed.'

Daisy shook her head. 'There's Jacques.' She indicated a small, dark-haired French boy. 'He's the best swimmer, but I raced him and I won.'

'OK, but not too long, the barbecue . . . ' but the two children were already racing up the pool.

'Your daughter?' Jake handed Fleur a towel. 'She's a great swimmer for one so young.'

'She loves the water, although there's not much opportunity in London. But she's loving it here.' She wrapped herself in the towel. 'I must go and change and get Daisy ready for the barbecue.'

Jake watched her as she rubbed her hair dry. 'Can we talk?' he said.

'Why sure, just let me go in the house and change and then get Daisy out of the pool.'

Fleur ran into the house to where Jean Pierre and his wife, Marie, had set aside a room for guests. She changed into dark trousers and a white and silver top and with a quick dab of make-up, she was back to collect Daisy.

'I won, Mummee, I beat Jacques.' Daisy was dancing up and down in triumph.

'Good race,' Jake said.

'I'll take her.' Wanda was now by the pool. 'There's a children's party organised in the orchard.'

Jake and Fleur were left alone. The pool was empty of swimmers now, and stars were just beginning to twinkle in the evening sky.

'Well,' Jake said, 'yet another coincidence. What are you doing here?'

'I'm a friend of the Dubois family, Celeste especially. And you?'

'Same, a friend of Celeste's.'

Just then, the woman Fleur had seen with Jake at the market came hurrying towards them. 'Jake, quickly, over here. That guy I told you about, owns the

Chateau de Puis, wants to talk to you. Jean Pierre asked him to the barbecue to meet you.. Come on, Jake, this is important.' She gave a cursory nod towards Fleur then pulled at Jake's arm. 'Hurry!'

Jake frowned. 'Just a minute . . . '

'Now!' the woman said.

'See you later,' Jake said to Fleur. And that was the last she saw of him that evening.

* * *

The barbecue was a great success; Fleur couldn't remember how long it was since she'd had such a good time. Well after midnight, Tim offered to see Fleur and Daisy home. Daisy promptly fell fast asleep in the back of the car.

'I think we've cracked it,' Tim said, 'a few finishing touches and you'll be ready to go. Any more problems from your stepfather?'

'A few letters from his lawyers, but Celeste reckons it's all over. He's still making threatening noises, and he hasn't personally shown up at the Manoir, but . . . ' She hesitated. 'This will sound completely paranoid, Tim, but, well, I have a feeling I . . . we . . . are being watched. The same car is frequently outside the Manoir, and I've had a couple of strange phone calls. I answer, there's a pause, then the phone's put down. But maybe I am just being paranoid. I just so much want this to be a success, Tim. And you've helped so much.'

'It's a pleasure. You know, Fleur, I have to go back to England next week and . . . well . . . I really don't want to.'

'Could it be that Celeste has something to do with that?'

'Well . . . would you mind? You know how I've always felt about you. I know I've never had a hope, but . . . '

'Tim, you are one of my dearest friends and I think you and Celeste are perfect for each other.'

'I hope you're right! And now, here's your Dinky Dolly House. How long before you're open for business, by the way?'

'Not long, within the next week or so. The publicity is out tomorrow.'

Carefully, Tim lifted Daisy from the car. 'I'll carry her in. Good job you left the lights on.'

'But I didn't. I remember switching everything off.'

'I'd better come in with you,' Tim frowned. 'You take Daisy.'

Cautiously, they went up the stone steps to the cottage. The front porch light was on, also a bedroom light.

'I must have made a mistake. Sorry, Tim, it was a bit hectic this morning. It seems an age since we left for the barbecue. Do you want coffee?'

'No, thanks. See you at the Manoir tomorrow. There are just a few finishing touches to be done.'

Fleur shivered. 'I'm a bit scared, Tim. Have I done the right thing? Will Daisy be happy here? How will I ever pay off my loans? Will Stefan's bistro be a success? Will . . . ?'

Tim hugged her, 'You and Daisy will love it here, and Stefan's bistro will be the talk of Brittany.'

★ ★ ★

After Tim had gone, Fleur settled Daisy into bed and checked her mobile phone. There was a message from Jake Merton. 'Sorry, Fleur, got tied up tonight. How about lunch tomorrow or the next day? I'll ring you.'

Lunch with Jake . . . Fleur's last sleepy thought was, how had he got her mobile number?

Only a couple of hours later she woke with a start, but everything was quiet. Then there was a faint cry from Daisy in the next bed. She had outgrown her cot and was in her own bed in Fleur's room. Fleur went over to the bed and tucked the covers around her little girl.

She was about to creep back into her own bed when some instinct drew her to the window. Although the cottage was quite some way from the Manoir,

Fleur's bedroom window overlooked a corner of the main building and the nearby chapel. She caught her breath.

Lights were on in the chapel, lights which had been off when she and Tim had driven back from the barbecue. She remembered, because Tim had made some remark about his tools and their safety in the old chapel. As she watched, the lights went out and seconds later, a car engine revved. Fleur could just make out its tail lights as it drove off.

But one light remained on in the chapel.

Fleur's watch showed 3.30 a.m. Impossible for any of the building workers to still be there at such an hour. As she watched, the light went out and, in the bright moonlight, she saw two figures leaving the chapel. Two minutes later, car lights swept down the drive and away from the Manoir.

A Startling Confession

Fleur dragged herself out of a deep sleep. Daisy was holding her mobile which was chirruping away. 'Mummy,' Daisy gave her the phone.

'Thank you, love . . . what time . . . ?' To Fleur's horror it was half past nine. She should have been at the Manoir at least an hour ago. there were so many jobs to be done before the opening. 'Hello . . . '

'Hi Fleur, it's Jake. I left a message.'

'Oh, yes, sorry. I've only just woken up.'

'I'm so sorry I didn't get back to see you again at the barbecue.'

'That's OK. It was a good party, but I'm really late for work now.'

'But you're the boss, aren't you?'

'Well, that's a bit irrelevant as things

are. There's so much still to do.'

'So, can you take a lunch break? There's a lovely place by the river, near the coast.'

'Jake, I can't possibly. I've so much to do.'

'Tonight then. Dinner?'

'I try to spend time with Daisy in the evening.'

'Later in the evening?'

'Well, maybe. Wanda could stay with Daisy, I suppose.'

'Late evening it is, then. I'll pick you up at the Manoir. What time?'

'How do you know where I am?' Fleur asked, frowning.

There was a small pause. 'I asked around at the barbecue. Everyone there seemed to know all about you.'

'And who gave you my mobile number?'

'Ah.'

'So, how . . . ?'

'Fleur, I'll come clean and tell you tonight. Please . . . '

'All right. I expect you know where the Manoir is.'

'I do, actually. Look forward to seeing you later, Fleur.'

As she switched off her phone, Fleur felt a small shiver run through her. She didn't know if it was apprehension or expectation.

'Mum?' Daisy gave her a poke.

'Sorry, love. Breakfast, sorry. I'll get up now.'

There was a note from Wanda on the table. *Left you both to sleep. Am at the Manoir.*

After breakfast, Fleur and Daisy walked across the parkland towards the Manoir. In the Spring sunshine it looked like a different building from when they'd first arrived: newly painted shutters flanked the tall windows now sparkling reflected sunshine; the terrace, flagged with new slabs, was swept clean, tables and chairs were stacked against the chapel walls ready for arranging. The chapel! Fleur suddenly remembered the previous night. As she hurried towards the building, Celeste came to meet her.

'Sorry, I'm late. I overslept,' Fleur said.

'Don't apologise. You've worked so hard.'

'Everyone's here, then?'

'Of course. Uncle Jean Pierre's gang are already on to the clearing away process and, as you see, the chapel's empty now.'

'Is it? I thought I saw someone in there very late last night. Lights were on, there were cars.'

'Are you sure?'

'Certain.'

'I can't think who that could have been. Maybe one of the builders fetching his tools?'

'Funny time to do that.'

'Well, it's all in order in there now.'

'Maybe I dreamt it.' She waved to Jean Pierre who was walking up from the main gate.

'Bonjour, Fleur.' He took her arm and winked at Celeste.

'He wants to show you something, then I want to talk to you.'

'What about?' Fleur asked.

'Something extraordinary,' was all Celeste would say.

Jean Pierre had a firm grip on Fleur's elbow and was practically pushing her down the drive towards the road. He stopped at the gate.

Fleur gasped. There it was, a painted sign which announced to the world: Manoir de Belvoir.

Wanda, with Daisy, and Celeste had followed Fleur and Jean Pierre.

'Jean Pierre would like to add a coat of arms to the sign. I think the Remondins did possess one once,' Celeste said.

'Really? I know so little of the Remondin history,' Fleur told her.

'Time for that later. Next week you will be truly open.'

'I'd like to have a small thank you party just before we open, get Stefan to cook up some surprises.'

'OK, I'll tell him,' Wanda smiled. 'How about the day before we open? Friday night?'

'That's only five days away.' Fleur looked panic-stricken.

'It'll be fine. Come on, Daisy, let's help Stefan.'

Daisy went off happily clutching Wanda's hand.

'She loves it here so much, Celeste. I just hope it'll work out,' Fleur said with a frown.

Celeste took Fleur's arm. 'I'm sure it will. But I have some news for you.'

'What? Is it Paul Maynard?'

'No, he's gone quiet lately. No, it's an offer for the Manoir.'

'An offer? But how? Why? The Manoir's not for sale.'

'I know that, but as your agent I'm obliged to pass the offer on. It's an anonymous buyer working for a big property developer.'

Celeste gave Fleur a figure that made her gasp. 'It's never worth anything like that!'

'It is to a developer. Look at the land you have here, and so close to the town.'

'It couldn't be Paul Maynard, could it?'

'Not for that sum of money, I wouldn't have thought.'

'I don't want to sell, this is my family home.'

'Well Fleur, I admire you for that, but you could have a life of ease if you sold at the price this buyer is prepared to offer.'

'I don't care. Please tell your anonymous would-be buyer that the Manoir de Belvoir is not for sale.'

'I surely will. Now, I will take Tim to the ferry. But he will come back at the weekend. For the party, of course.'

'Oh, for the party? No other reason of course?'

'Of course not.' But Celeste's blush told a different story.

* * *

At the end of that day, Fleur felt for the first time that they might just be ready to open for business the following week.

Suddenly everything was slotting into place; the en-suite guest rooms were fully fitted down to the last set of fluffy bath towels and quality soaps and shampoos; cleaners had polished the floors to mirror quality, and Babette Remondin's furniture now stood in its rightful place and looked thoroughly at home.

Fleur and Daisy went from room to room, the little girl quite awed by the elegance of their surroundings and, for the first time, Fleur had the rather sad thought that she would have liked to live at the Manoir with her own family. 'Oh Ben,' she breathed softly, 'you should be here with us instead of strangers living in our lovely house.' But of course, common sense and reason prevailed. Fleur knew the Manoir had to be a business to provide herself and Daisy with a living.

Even with the sale of her London flat she was up to her neck in debt.

The Manoir *had* to pay its way.

Back at the cottage, Wanda and Daisy watched Fleur get ready to go out.

'It's only a quick drink,' she said, as Wanda gave Daisy a nudge. 'Haven't seen that top before, have we, Daisy?'

'No. It's pretty.'

'Isn't it?'

'I'll be sad to leave here,' Fleur tried to change the subject, 'but we need to be over at the house, and the cottage has been let out for the summer.'

'Mummy does look pretty, doesn't she Daisy?' Wanda grinned.

Fortunately, the bell rang at that point announcing that Jake was at the door.

'Shan't be long. See you soon.'

'Aren't you going to ask him in?' said Wanda, but Fleur was already out of the door.

★　★　★

Jake indicated the Manoir as they drove towards the gate. 'It's quite beautiful and the grounds are fantastic,' he said.

'Practical too, I hope. A business as well as a home.'

'I'm sure it will be. When are you opening?'

'Saturday. Five day's time.'

'Really? You've worked a miracle.'

'Not me; Jean Pierre, Celeste, Tim. We're having a small party on Friday, a celebration.'

'Am I invited?'

'Oh. Well, what about your . . . um . . . wife . . . girlfriend?' Up until this point, Fleur had completely forgotten about the bossy woman Jake had been with at the barbecue. What a fool she was. 'I shouldn't be going out with you,' she said.

'Fleur Weston, what do you think I am? I don't have a wife or a girlfriend. Amanda is my personal assistant who is, in fact, married with two small children at home in America.'

'Oh.'

'And she can't wait to get back home, that's why she was pushing me to close that deal.'

'Oh, sorry.' Fleur glanced at Jake Merton — his strong profile, capable hands on the wheel, dark blond hair, and her stomach felt sort of wobbly, something she hadn't felt for a long time. 'What do you do then, work, I mean?' she asked. 'And how do you know my name is Weston? And how do you know my mobile number?'

'Ssh, just enjoy the scenery. Once we're at the restaurant, I'll come clean, I promise. Nearly there now.'

As river gave way to sea, a tiny restaurant sat facing the water. A terrace with tables and chairs caught the last rays of the setting sun.

'It's lovely,' Fleur said.

'We could have a glass of wine out here and go inside to eat?' Jake suggested.

'Fine. It seems a shame to miss the sunset, and it's still warm.'

'I agree. I'll bring out the menu.' In

no time, he had returned with two glasses of wine. 'I've ordered the bouillibaise, I hope that's OK. I can change it if you like.'

'No, that'll be fine.'

Jake sat down and raised his glass. 'Here's to the Manoir de Belvoir. And success.'

'Thank you.' Fleur sipped her wine. 'I hope it is a success. So much depends on it. This is an enormous change and I worry whether I've done the right thing by Daisy.'

'From what I've seen of Daisy, she seems to have adapted like a native.'

'Yes, she has, thank goodness. Thank you for bringing me here, Jake. I probably needed to get away for a short time, put things into perspective.'

The sun was now a huge orange ball hovering over the horizon. 'Let's watch it set,' Fleur said, 'and you can tell me how you know my name and how you came to be at the Dubois barbecue.'

'I told you, Celeste invited me.'

'How do you know Celeste?'

'Through work. And as for your name, you told me on the stairs, remember?'

'I did?'

'Well, you muttered something. I confess I wasn't quite sure what you said, so I went back upstairs and asked your friend, Jane. She was a bit cagey at first but she'd already met my father so she thought it would be OK.'

'But why did you want to know about me?'

Jake twisted his glass around. 'Because I knew I'd have you on my mind.' He paused to let Fleur digest this startling confession. 'Jane told me you were a widow and that you had a little girl and a job in the city. She told me also about the Manoir.'

Fleur was silent.

'You're not going to be angry with Jane, are you? It took a while to convince her my intentions were honourable. Fleur, look at me, that moment on the stairs, there was something between us. You felt it too, didn't you?'

He took her hand and held it across the table, his eyes never leaving hers, and Fleur couldn't look away. She felt warmth spreading through her, a warmth that could reach her heart if she let it. 'I'm not sure, Jake. My husband, Ben is . . . has, been with me in spirit for so long. I can't forget him, I can't.'

'I wouldn't ever want you to. He's Daisy's father and he was your husband. But would he want you to go through the rest of your life, unloved, on your own?'

'I haven't thought about that. Since the accident he's always been in my heart, every day.'

'How long since your husband died?'

'Nearly three years. It was a car accident coming home from work. There was fog, a jack-knifed lorry, a pile up . . . ' Her voice broke.

Jake reached for her other hand. 'Don't, Fleur. I'm sorry, I shouldn't have asked. It's too early.'

'No, no, I'm fine. Really. And you're

right. Ben would have hated me to spend my life mourning for him. It's just . . . we had so little time together, and he never knew Daisy. I was seven month's pregnant when he died.'

'That must have been hard.'

'Yes, but I had Daisy. I had a little bit of Ben in her, and I wasn't alone.' She shivered as the sun sank down into the sea.

A woman came out of the restaurant. 'Monsieur Merton, bouillibaise.'

'Do you feel like eating, Fleur?'

'I do.' She wiped her eyes. 'Sorry, Jake.'

'What for? I'm glad you came tonight and I'm glad we talked about Ben.'

* * *

The bouillibaise was magnificent, the restaurant warm and friendly. Jake talked about his home in San Diego, Fleur told him about her job at Simkins in London. They both deliberately avoided the personal. Fleur felt a door had opened just a crack but she wasn't yet ready to push it further.

When they arrived back at the cottage, Stefan was there with Wanda. 'Nothing wrong?' Fleur asked anxiously. Stefan so rarely left his bistro where, as his opening day grew nearer, he had so much to do.

'No problems,' Wanda said. 'Daisy's fast asleep. Stefan came to check on the pre-opening party menu. He is anxious it goes well. It would be a good omen.'

'It'll be fine, you're not to worry. And I don't need to see the menu, Stefan, just keep it fairly simple,' Fleur said, and yawned. 'Sorry, I'm a bit tired. Thank you for this evening, Jake.'

'My pleasure.' He dropped a light kiss on Fleur's cheek and smiled at Wanda and Stefan before leaving.

Wanda looked at Fleur. 'You had a good time tonight?'

'Yes I did. Jake Merton is a nice man.'

Opening Night

Fleur closed the door of La Maison de Jardinier with regret. She'd loved the time she'd spent there in the little cottage with Daisy and Wanda but now, the day before the official opening, they were moving into the Manoir itself. Three attic rooms had been converted into temporary living quarters. Later, if the venture was a success, the attics would be turned into a deluxe en-suite apartment for Fleur and Daisy.

Now no longer a building site, but an elegant, gracious country house, the Manoir sat in a sweeping parkland garden. The transformation was truly staggering. Spring shrubs graced the lawns and the large vegetable garden would provide Stefan with the fresh organic produce for his kitchen. Georges, the young, enthusiastic gardener, gave Fleur a cheery wave. She noticed he had boxes full of early potatoes.

She crossed behind the vegetable garden towards a small copse of shrubs and trees.

Fleur was intrigued by this part of the grounds, because it was here that she had come across, of all things, a grave, a few weeks earlier. Now she read the headstone which was simply engraved:

Yvette Remondin
b. 1901 — d. 1944
'Mon amour.'

Fleur had been startled by her find, no-one had ever mentioned a grave in the grounds of the Manoir, and when she had asked Celeste and various older Dubois family members about it, they had looked puzzled. The general consensus was that the death had occurred in wartime and so many things had happened then. Sadly, Yvette Remondin's life and death seemed to have made no local impression.

One day, Fleur promised herself she'd find time to explore the Remondin history. For now, the grave would be a private place where she could stand in peace and quiet and wonder about her ancestor. More and more she was tugged by her roots and she believed that, as a Remondin, she truly belonged to the Manoir.

★   ★   ★

It was a lovely early summer evening. Guests began to arrive, all dressed for the important local occasion, the re-opening of Remondin Manoir.

Jake Merton arrived with champagne and his personal assistant, Amanda. 'Hope you don't mind. Amanda's worried about her children, caught some sort of bug. She's fretting for us to go home.'

'And are you going?' Fleur asked.

He smiled. 'I've still a lot to do in the UK, particularly in London where I'm staying in one of the flats where you used to be.' He poured champagne into their glasses. 'Now, I have a surprise for you. Follow me.'

Jake took Fleur's hand.

'Where are we going?'

'You'll see.' He led her towards the chapel, which had been cleared to accommodate guests in more comfortable chairs.

Jake switched the lights on.

'Hi, Fleur! Surprise!' Jane held out her arms to Fleur.

'How wonderful! Sam, too, and Alice. But when I phoned you, Jane, you said you couldn't make it.'

'It was your friend, Jake, who fixed it. He organised everything. It was all a bit last minute.'

'Jake arranged it?'

'Well, we were going to come out later but he's a persuasive guy. He thought it would be a good idea if we were your very first paying guests.'

'Oh, you can't possibly pay. But how long can you stay?'

'Just a weekend for now,' Sam said,

'and we're heading right back home unless we pay. Your first paying guests, maybe we'll bring you luck. But from what I've seen so far, you don't need it. It's a dream, Fleur.'

'I can't wait to see it all,' Jane said, 'I don't know how you've managed to do it in such a short time.'

'With lots of help,' Fleur grinned. 'Yes, Alice, we'll go and find Daisy. And then there will be fireworks in the orchard by the vegetable garden.'

'A vegetable garden! Organic, of course? See, Sam, this is country living for you,' Jane said.

'Hardly country living. This is right by the town, though you wouldn't know it. Fabulous location, Fleur.'

'It is, isn't it? Where's your luggage? I'll put you in our best deluxe en-suite.'

'I should hope so,' Sam laughed.

* * *

Alice was pulling her mother in the direction of the orchard as everyone

124

headed for the fireworks display.

Jake made to follow them but Fleur caught his arm. 'Jake, thank you, that was such a wonderful surprise.'

'I'm glad you're pleased. I did wonder if I was doing the right thing but I got to know Jane and Sam well when I was in London and they talked about you such a lot. I knew they wanted to come out and see you.'

Fleur reached up to his cheek, but he turned his head and her mouth met his. Shock, surprise, a hesitation, then Jake kissed her, holding her close.

'Fleur?' he questioned softly, then kissed her again.

She found it natural and easy to respond, to hold him close. It had been so long . . . then . . .

'Jake, we should be going. You have an early appointment, don't forget. Oh, I'm sorry,' but the woman's voice was angry, not apologetic.

Jake frowned. 'For goodness' sake, Amanda.'

'OK. Right. I'll leave, I can get a taxi.

I need to phone home again, Dwight's not well. Sorry,' she said to Fleur, 'I'm just worried about my little boy.'

'Sure, no problem, I have to see to my friends who've just arrived.' Fleur turned to Jake. 'Thank you again, very thoughtful of you, I appreciate it,' and before he could say anything, she ran across the lawn towards the firework display where the bonfire was shooting tongues of orange flame up to the starry summer sky.

*   *   *

The fire was almost spent and the partygoers were leaving in a reluctant trickle, tired children carried sleepily in their parents' arms. Celeste and Tim, Fleur, Jane and Sam, remained on the terrace for a final nightcap. Wanda was putting Daisy and Alice to bed, Stefan, exhausted but well pleased with the reception of his Polish cuisine, joined the party on the terrace.

'It went well? You're pleased, Fleur?'

he asked anxiously.

'Of course, Stefan, it couldn't have gone better. Thanks for all your hard work.'

'It's only the beginning, the next few weeks will be the test.'

'It's really lovely,' Jane said eagerly, 'our room's a dream and I can't believe . . . ' She stopped as a car came sweeping up the drive. 'Looks as though someone's forgotten something.'

Fleur hoped it might be Jake; he'd completely disappeared.

The car stopped, and a man got out and came up the steps towards them. 'Hello, sorry it's a bit late but we were on our way from the south. We got a bit delayed. Any chance of a room for the night? We saw your sign.'

Fleur leapt to her feet. 'Of course, of course. Please, do come in. We are in operation. Please.'

'Thanks. Peter and Mary Browning. I'll get the bags,' and Fleur's first real life guest went back to his car.

'I can't believe this,' Fleur said,

tidying up plates and glasses, 'a customer already! Tim, would you mind showing Mr Browning where to put the car? Stefan, could you rustle up a supper tray?'

'Sure.'

Fleur still looked stunned. 'This is all a bit sudden, but it's surely a good omen. Thanks everybody,' she said, as she went down the steps to greet her first paying guests, and tried to forget about Jake's abrupt departure.

* * *

The following days were spent supervising the staff, taking bookings, keeping up with the paperwork. The business side was no problem, that was Fleur's field, but the actual running of what, in essence, was a small hotel, was a different matter. She needed all her tact and diplomacy to iron out a few teething problems but as the days passed her confidence grew. Her hostess skills blossomed and she began to enjoy her new, very different, lifestyle.

Jake had e-mailed to say he was in Scotland on business but would be returning to Brittany before he left for London and the States. Fleur hesitated before replying. Her heart was touched, she recognised and admitted that, but she was wary, too. Jake was still something of a mystery. She'd bide her time.

Buoyed up by the complimentary remarks in her guest book, she began to think she had made the right decision about the Manoir. Then, several weeks after she'd opened, her stepfather arrived.

She and Daisy had been picking strawberries in the vegetable garden. Their trugs were full, though more had gone in Daisy's mouth than in her mini-trug. 'Stefan will want to make a lovely dessert, so I wouldn't eat any more, Daisy,' Fleur was saying, before her heart sank as she saw a familiar black car by the house.

As Fleur approached the terrace,

Paul Maynard and his son, Rob, were coming out of the chapel.

'Good morning, Fleur, and little Daisy, too. Hasn't she grown? France obviously suits her, and you too, Fleur, my dear. You're looking very well,' Paul declared.

'Hello,' Fleur responded without enthusiasm, 'what are you doing here? Are you just passing through?' she added hopefully.

'Well, that depends. Our plans are fluid but I thought it wise to keep an eye on the Manoir. See what you've done with it.'

'As you see, it's a thriving business.'

'Indeed, and I haven't come to interfere.'

'So why have you come then?'

'Just to remind you I do have an interest in my late wife's property.'

'You are quite free to take an interest, but you have no legal right here.'

'Well, I think you might just be mistaken about that. Rob, have you my lawyer's letter?'

'It's here, Dad, but . . . '

'The letter, please, Rob.'

Rob passed a document to Fleur.

'No need to read it now,' Paul said, 'but be sure to peruse it at your leisure. In essence, it says that as the surviving spouse of my marriage to my dear Babette, I have a right to the Manoir under French law. And in the light of that, it would be foolish not to keep an eye on the property as is my legal right, wouldn't you say, Fleur?'

'I am sure you have no rights at all. But I will pass this on to my lawyers,' Fleur said coolly.

'That is your right, of course. I don't wish any ill-feeling between us, but I shall be visiting from time to time, not least to see how you and my grand-daughter are getting on. I'm most impressed by what I've seen already.'

'I can't prevent you from visiting but I'm going to run my business my own way without any interference.'

'I wouldn't dream of interfering! But I wonder, do you have any plans to convert the chapel?'

'The chapel? Well, no. It's used for storage at present.'

'It would make a lovely holiday cottage.'

'I'm sure,' Fleur said, 'but I've enough to do at present.'

'We'll be on our way, then. Paris is our next stop. Goodbye, Fleur, I expect we'll be seeing you again very soon. Daisy, here's some pocket money from Grandad.'

Daisy's eyes widened as Paul Maynard dropped some notes into her hand. 'Thank you,' she said, looking at Fleur.

Her mother nodded reluctantly and Daisy tucked the money away in her pocket and blew a kiss to Paul as he went back to his car.

'Rob, what's going on?' Fleur asked, as Rob went to follow his father. Fleur had always got on with Rob whenever they'd met, and he struck her as a complete contrast to her stepfather.

'I'm not sure,' Rob frowned, 'I can't

quite fathom his interest in the Manoir. I don't honestly think he wants to make a claim on it, but for some reason he wants right of access.'

'He doesn't want to buy me out or anything?'

'I don't think so, otherwise he'd have offered before now. It's not his type of property deal, though this must be a very valuable site for development if you could ever get planning permission. Perfect real estate.'

Fleur shuddered. 'Don't dare even to think it. Do you know, we're almost already booked through to the autumn? So why can't Paul just leave me alone?'

Rob shook his head. 'I don't know, he's developed a kind of obsession about the place. He's not been very well lately. But you look great, Fleur. It obviously suits you here.'

'Well, I am out and about instead of being stuck in front of a computer most of the day.'

'We should see more of each other.'

'And you should move out of your

father's shadow, Rob.'

'Maybe,' Rob laughed ruefully. 'Anyway, take the letter, show it to your lawyer. I think it's just Dad's excuse to keep an eye on the Manoir.'

An irate summons from the car made Rob smile. 'Habit of a lifetime, Fleur. Take care and good luck.'

It was only later that Fleur realised she hadn't queried the missing furniture from the warehouse.

A Stranger Puzzles Fleur

Fleur was so busy she forgot about Paul Maynard's veiled threats. Her hard-working staff, several with Dubois connections, took a personal interest in the Manoir and there was a wonderful atmosphere of goodwill and camaraderie. Comments in the guest book were complimentary, only a couple of visitors expressing reservations about Polish cooking in France. Stefan took note and re-balanced his menus more in favour of French cuisine.

One sunny afternoon in late June, Fleur and Daisy went to the vegetable garden to pick salad leaves and strawberries. Georges Dubois, working in one of the glass houses he'd restored, beckoned them over. An old man was seated in a cane basket chair by the entrance. Georges introduced him. 'This is my great-grandfather, Henri Dubois. He heard you were interested in the grave in the copse. He can tell you the story if you're interested.'

'I certainly am,' Fleur replied. 'Thank you, Georges.'

'It is a little sad, Yvette's story, for a small girl. Maybe Daisy can help me with some watering?'

'That's thoughtful. Thank you, Georges.'

Daisy was only too pleased to scamper away with a small watering can and follow Georges between the rows of flourishing tomato plants.

The old man in the wicker chair stood up to greet Fleur and took her hand. 'Madame Weston, I'm pleased to meet you, I've heard such a lot about your enterprise. I hope it goes well. I used to work here many years ago when it was called Manoir Remondin.'

'Really? When did the name change?' Fleur hadn't noticed that when she'd studied the deeds.

'Oh, a long time ago, when the

Remondins were flourishing. A little after the end of The First World War. I was in charge of the stables here then. I would have liked to have joined up but of course I was too young. Most of the horses had gone to the front. So many were killed in that war, brave horses as well as brave soldiers. The war virtually brought an end to the Remondin line.'

'Please, sit down,' Fleur said. 'I'm glad to talk to you. I know so little about my family Remondin.'

The man sat back in his chair, blue eyes still keen and alert in spite of his age. 'I'm pleased to see a Remondin here again. You are Babette's daughter?'

Fleur nodded and leaned forward eagerly. 'Do you know of any other Remondins? Another branch in France, perhaps?'

Henri Dubois shook his head, scrutinising her face before answering, 'I see the Remondin in you, there are no others.'

'Oh. What about Yvette in the grave? Were there no children?'

'No. She married the last of the Remondins, Raoul, who was born at the end of the war in 1918, a week after the Armistice. The poor baby, his pappy never came home. He lies forever in Flanders Fields.'

'But Raoul?'

'Brought up by the women left at the Manoir. Spoilt, of course, but a good man for all that.'

'And Yvette?' Fleur could see Henri's eyes closing, the sun in the enclosed garden was soporific. He yawned, 'Mmm, a girl from the Dordogne, Southern France, Raoul married her in 1938. Not treated too well in the war by the Remondins. She was not popular, not a local girl. She died in 1944. Influenza, I believe. Pregnant too, so they say.'

'How terrible.'

'Aye, and young Raoul was never the same after that. He had her buried in the garden as you saw, then he went off to war himself. Killed in Africa.'

'How dreadful. But no-one in the

town seems to know the story.'

'Well, in those days the Remondin women kept themselves pretty much to themselves. There was a decline in the family fortunes. No heads for business, you see. The men were merchants in the old days in the nineteenth century, they were very prosperous, did lots for the town and district . . . '

'Mummy, Mummy, come and see!' Daisy's excited voice broke in.

'What is it?' Fleur saw Henri's chin sink on to his chest and a gentle snoring told her that was all the Remondin history she would get that afternoon.

Looking at the peaceful, sunlit garden, it was difficult to imagine those war-torn years, although there was a memorial in the town square in memory of the townspeople who had helped the Maquis resistance.

'Mummy, see, Georges gave me some 'mato plants to look after. Oh, the old man asleep?' Daisy tip-toed nearer, peering at Henri's face, wrinkled with age. 'Very old,' she whispered.

'He is, and tired. Let's tiptoe away and leave him in peace. Show me your tomato plants.'

But before Fleur could examine Daisy's gardening project, the receptionist came running across the lawn. 'Fleur, there's a gentleman in Reception. New arrival. Wants to speak particularly to you. Sorry.'

'Don't be, I'm just coming. Georges, is it OK if Daisy stays here for a few minutes? And thank you for letting me talk to your great-grandfather.'

'I'm sure he enjoyed talking to you. I'm afraid we young ones are often too busy to listen to his tales of the past.'

'I know, it's a shame. I'm sure your great-grandfather holds the key to lots of mysteries from the past, especially about the Manoir.'

Georges shrugged, 'Maybe, but the past's gone, isn't it? It's the here and now and the future I'm concerned about. That's the way, Daisy, pick out the side shoots — very good.' He beamed at Fleur. 'We'll make a

140

horticulturist of her yet.'

'She could do a lot worse,' Fleur smiled, as she hurried back to the Manoir.

★   ★   ★

The reception area was empty except for a man who was examining some photos Tim had taken of the building before and after reconstruction.

'Can I help you? Aimee said you wanted to speak to me. I'm Fleur Weston.'

The man remained staring at the photographs on the wall.

'Sir?' Fleur tapped him on the shoulder. 'You wanted to speak to me,' she repeated patiently. 'I'm Fleur Weston, the Manoir's owner. Did you want to book a room?'

The man turned round and stared at her, then coughed. 'Sorry, I haven't been well. I thought . . . a few days . . . a day . . . in the country would be pleasant.'

'So it's a room. One night?'

'For now, yes.'

'I do have a room for tonight and our restaurant is open if you want to book supper.'

'Restaurant? Um, oh yes.'

'And it's just yourself?' Fleur, behind the desk, scanned the computer screen.

'Myself? Oh yes. Thank you.' He looked at her again. She returned his scrutiny, puzzled by his manner. Difficult to tell his age, anywhere between fifty and sixty, greying hair, still thick and wavy, piercing stare, deep grey eyes, and, Fleur thought, something familiar about his expression. Very well dressed. 'So, you'd like to book in for tonight, Mr . . . er?'

'Oh yes. And I'm sorry, but I'm not too clear about my plans for the next few days.'

'I'll book you in for this evening and you can take pot luck if you decide to stay longer. Your room is free for the days following but if someone else comes along . . . '

142

'I understand, thank you. That'll be fine.'

Fleur turned the guest book towards him, 'Could you register please, Mr . . . '

He took the pen, hesitated, scrawled something undecipherable, then added, British, Hampstead, London.

'Thank you. Do you need help with your luggage?'

'No, thank you, I only have one bag and my laptop.'

'Right. I'll show you to your room.'

'No, no, just point me in the right direction.'

'Should I send up tea, coffee?' Fleur was puzzled, there was something very odd about this guest, but she couldn't put her finger on it.

'Thank you, no. I have to go out into the town.'

'And dinner this evening?'

'Most probably. Possibly.'

'Well, I hope you enjoy your visit to the Manoir de Belvoir. Enjoy the grounds. Complimentary drinks will be served on the terrace before dinner, weather permitting.'

'Yes.' For the first time he looked directly at her. 'There's always that, the weather I mean. My room?'

'First floor, turn left, number six. Ring down if there's anything at all you might want.' Fleur looked at the register again. 'Mr . . . ?'

'Thank you.' The man picked up his bag and went quickly up the stairs.

'Sorry, Fleur.' Aimee, the on-duty receptionist came into the hall, 'He wouldn't deal with me, insisted on speaking to you. A bit odd, don't you think?'

'I suppose so. He certainly didn't give anything away, even his name.' She showed Aimee the guest book.

'Goodness. It's impossible, worse than a doctor's writing, and his address, just Hampstead, London. Hey, perhaps he is a doctor. How long's he staying?'

'No idea. He did seem a bit strange, but never mind, so long as he pays his bill!'

★ ★ ★

Fleur went back to the vegetable garden to claim her leaves and strawberries and to collect Daisy. The old man had gone.

'My sister picked him up,' Georges told her. 'He's quite frail now but we all look after him, and he enjoyed talking to you. Here's Daisy, quite the little gardener. Maybe I can teach you about the flowers?'

'Yes, please. Now water my 'matoes?'

'Tomorrow, maybe,' Fleur said. 'Thank you, Georges. I'll take these to Stefan right away.'

Stefan was delighted with the strawberries. 'Perfect. Georges is a good gardener.'

'And you're doing a great job here,' Fleur said.

'I love it, I love the Manoir, I love Brittany. I could live here for ever.'

'And Wanda?'

'She loves it, too, Fleur, and we'd like to get married soon. Could we be married here, do you think?'

'What, now?'

Stefan grinned. 'No, maybe at the end of the season.'

'Well, that's up to you and Wanda. I'd be very pleased, but what about your friends and family in Poland?'

'No problem. We could hire a coach, bus them over.'

Fleur laughed. 'Stefan, you are amazing, nothing seems to trouble you, does it?'

'No. And I have plans for the Manoir, maybe a cookery school in the Autumn, Christmas banquets . . . '

Fleur put her hands to her ears. 'Stop, stop, Stefan! Let's just get this first season over.'

'Right, OK, but the wedding?'

'Sure, make your plans. Just let me know.'

Stefan smiled. 'Thank you. Now, I have a large party booking for tonight, the local archery club. They especially asked for some Polish dishes.' Stefan picked up the baskets of strawberries. 'These will make marvellous Pavlovas. Thanks, Fleur.'

* * *

It was afternoon before Fleur got back to her office. Daisy was at a friend's birthday party, and Wanda was helping Stefan in the kitchen. She settled down to some paperwork, first checking her e-mails. There were several from suppliers, one from Tim, who said he was returning to Brittany, and, to Fleur's delight, bringing Jane and Alice with him. She instantly replied that she'd be delighted to see them all.

As she cleared the screen, her phone rang.

'Oh, hi, is that you, Fleur? This is Amanda, Jake Merton's P.A. He asked me to phone you to say he's left Scotland and he's on his way back to France. He'll be at the Manoir in a day or so. He's got a Paris proposition.'

'A Paris proposition? Amanda, if you don't mind me asking, what exactly is it you and Jake Merton do?'

There was a pause. 'Don't you know?'

'No. I'm just curious, but if it's top secret . . . '

'There's no secret about it. His job is what brought him to the Manoir.'

'The Manoir?'

'Sure. He had in mind a possible buy-out.'

'Buy out! He wants to buy the Manoir?'

'Not once he'd seen it. It's far too small. But if the estate and land could be sold as a lot, well, maybe . . . '

Fleur's brain reeled.

'It's the family business,' Amanda continued blithely. 'He's big in the States and he's looking to expand into Europe. Luxury hotels with sports spas — Merton Ltd. You must have heard of them with your business background. Jake's on a fact-finding trip to find potential for development. Didn't he tell you?'

'No, but thank you for telling me.'

'I didn't think it was a secret. Sorry.'

'Don't be. It explains a lot. Thanks.'

Fleur put the phone down and took a

deep breath. What a fool she'd been. Of course Jake wasn't interested in her as a person, merely as the owner of some real estate for corporate expansion. A wave of disappointment washed over her, then annoyance at her gullibility. She'd never for a moment thought Jake had an ulterior motive in finding her and getting to know her. But it was for his own business interests. And why hadn't her friend, Jane, told her about Jake's business? Maybe he'd kept his reason for being over here from her, too.

'Work,' Fleur said aloud, 'my Manoir, that's what matters.' But the deceit rankled and she'd make sure to be unavailable when Jake Merton was next in Brittany.

Fleur Is Worried About Paul Maynard

It was harder than Fleur imagined to forget Jake but, determined not to see him again, she e-mailed she was away on business when he proposed visiting. And she informed him the Manoir was not for sale at any price. He did not reply.

Fortunately, Tim's return to Brittany brought Jane and Alice and that helped a little to put Jake out of Fleur's mind. Whenever she could, she took time out with her friend, exploring the local beaches. The beautiful summer weather held for the visit and both Fleur and Daisy were sorry when it was time to take Jane and Alice back to the Roscoff ferry.

'It's been a lovely week,' Jane said, as their bags were brought out to them.

'We'll come back as often as you can put up with us, and when your season's over you'll come and visit us, won't you? We'll be in our new home in the country by then.'

'Oh, we'd love to, Jane but Wanda and Stefan's wedding is planned for the end of October,' Fleur said.

'After that, then?'

'That would be lovely. I'm sure I'll need a break by then!'

'Can't Alice stay now?' Daisy pleaded.

'Please, please,' Alice joined in.

'Not right now,' Jane told her daughter, 'but we'll all come again soon.'

'Do you promise?' Alice tugged at her mother's skirt.

'I promise. There you are Fleur, a firm booking!'

'Great . . . what's the matter?'

Jane was looking over towards the garden cottage. 'Who's that?' she asked.

'Ah, he's our mystery guest, came for one night last week but he's still here, so he's moving into the cottage.'

Now Jane was shading her eyes against the sun. 'He looks sort of familiar, but I can't see properly, the sun's so bright.'

'I shouldn't worry. He's English, keeps himself to himself, very vague as to how long he's staying here. A bit odd, but harmless, I reckon.'

'Hmm — anyway, I expect it'll come to me, I'll let you know if it does. By the way, have you seen Jake Merton since he was over here last time? He seemed very struck on you.'

Fleur's lips tightened. 'Jake Merton? He wasn't interested in me, Jane, just my property here.'

'Really? You could have fooled me.'

* * *

When Fleur and Daisy returned to the Manoir after seeing Jane off, she was surprised to find the mystery man on the terrace, his laptop open on the table, but when he saw Fleur he closed it immediately and stood up. He was more casually dressed than before, in lightweight trousers and open-necked shirt, with a light jacket on the back of his chair.

'Mrs Weston, would you join me, with your little girl for a coffee? It's such a lovely afternoon.' Today he appeared much more confident and at ease. He smiled at Daisy. 'This is your daughter? Could she have an ice-cream, perhaps?'

'Well,' Fleur hesitated. She frequently mingled with her guests before dinner when complimentary cocktails were served. That way, she could assess the satisfaction level of her customers and was ready to act on any suggestions they might make for further improvements. She always enjoyed the socialising hour but this time it was a direct personal invitation. She was about to plead pressure of work, but Daisy had already decided. 'Yes please,' she said, 'strawberry ice-cream,' and settled herself on the chair next to the visitor.

'Er, well, very quickly then. I am busy

and I need to see Stefan about the restaurant,' Fleur said.

'Yes. I've met Stefan. He's a fine cook.' The man addressed Daisy, 'Do you like his Polish food?'

'Stefan nice.'

'I'll go in and order.' Fleur stood up. 'Daisy?'

'I'll stay here,' Daisy announced.

'I'll look after her,' the stranger said.

'Well . . . I shan't be a second then.' Fleur practically sprinted indoors and flung at the startled Aimee in Reception, 'Coffee, strawberry ice cream, terrace, quick as you can.'

'OK, coming up.'

* * *

When Fleur got back to the terrace, Daisy was deep in conversation with the man, who was listening very carefully.

'Coffee's on its way,' Fleur said, brightly sitting down and eyeing the stranger warily.

154

'Mum,' Daisy said, 'strawberry ice-cream and then show him,' she indicated the stranger, 'my 'matoes.'

'I'm sure Mr . . . er . . . isn't interested in your tomatoes, Daisy. Just eat your ice cream when it arrives.'

Aimee arrived with a tray of coffee and cakes and a strawberry ice-cream. She looked at Fleur questioningly.

'Please bill my room,' the man said.

Once Aimee had left, there was silence. Fleur felt uncomfortable, very unsure where all this was leading.

'I hope you don't mind me taking up your time, Mrs Weston.'

'No, no but I do have a lot to do.'

'I'm sure, and I won't keep you. I'd like to congratulate you on your Manoir. Have you been here long?'

'No, only since this year. It's our first season.'

'I see from the photos in Reception you had a very big reconstruction task.'

'Yes. It was hard work.'

'But well worth the effort. You deserve to succeed here.'

'Thank you. Will you be staying here much longer?'

'A few days perhaps.'

'It's just that your accommodation is booked for next week.'

'I know. I shall leave on time.' He drank his coffee then said abruptly, 'You and Daisy are very much alike. And your husband . . . ?'

'I'm a widow,' Fleur said quickly, 'and we should be going now. Daisy, say thank you for the ice-cream. Sorry, I still haven't got your name.'

The man pulled a card from an expensive-looking leather wallet. CHRISTOPHER JONES, PROPERTY CONSULTANT, HAMPSTEAD, LONDON.

'No!' Fleur dropped the card on the table. 'I should have guessed. My property is not for sale, Mr Jones.'

'Please, Mrs Weston. I've no interest in your property, charming though it is. It was sheer coincidence I hit upon the Manoir. No, my area is renovation and restoration, that's why I was interested when I arrived.'

'It's not for sale,' Fleur repeated.

'And I don't want to buy it. I just,' suddenly his assurance deserted him, 'I just needed a holiday, a break.'

'All right,' Fleur conceded, 'but it seems quite a few others are interested in the Manoir and I repeat, I'm not selling.'

'I'm not surprised by the interest. However, I repeat, I'm not interested in buying it.'

Fleur believed him but she was still uneasy. She stood up. 'Thank you for the coffee and ice-cream. Come along now, Daisy.'

'My 'matoes.'

'Another day,' Christopher Jones said, 'when Mummy isn't so busy.'

⋆ ⋆ ⋆

Later, Celeste tried to reassure Fleur. 'He's genuine, your mystery man. I've checked him out and he is more of a renovator and restorer. That's why he's interested in what you've achicved at the Manoir.'

'OK, he's in the clear, but Celeste, do you remember that first offer you got ages ago? Who was that from?'

Celeste shrugged. 'Routine. Property developers are always on the lookout whenever a parcel of land comes up. You refused and I've heard nothing since. Don't worry, Fleur.'

She tried not to, but a further visit from Paul Maynard didn't go any way to reassuring her.

She recognised his black car in the drive very early one morning and again he was coming out of the chapel. This time Rob wasn't with him.

'Good morning, Fleur. Lovely day. I've come to see how you're getting on.'

'Very well, Paul. And you should have heard from my lawyers by now that you have no claim to the Manoir at all.'

'I have indeed heard from them and have to concede defeat.'

To Fleur's surprise, he looked unconcerned. 'So you've no reason to visit here?' she said.

'Only to see you, my dear, and little

Daisy. Family interest, just to keep an eye on things. Naturally my offer still stands. I can give you a good price, set you and Daisy up without all this hard work.'

Fleur sighed. 'Paul, thank you, but I am never going to sell Manoir de Belvoir to you or anybody else.'

For a split second fury glinted in his eyes and his mouth tightened, but he quickly regained his composure. 'I accept that, Fleur, but maybe a compromise? The chapel here would convert to a lovely holiday home, bringing in more income for you and Daisy. I am willing to finance that. It would be an excellent investment for me.'

'Paul, no! Please, I don't want you involved with the Manoir. Please, go away and leave me alone.'

An ugly anger suffused Paul Maynard's face. 'That's your final word?'

'It is. I don't want to fall out with you, but I'd rather you didn't come round here again.'

'All right. I'm going. But one day you'll see reason and come to me begging to take me up on my offer. And remember, through my wife, your mother, I have a moral right to this property!' He strode to his car, slammed the door and drove away, narrowly avoiding a car coming up towards the house.

Fleur closed her eyes, trying to regain control. Paul Maynard's angry departure had shaken her, his obsessive desire to claim an interest in her Manoir had frightened her. What did he want with it? He had other properties in the UK and in Spain. What was he up to? Head in hands, she slumped down on a chair on the terrace trying to shake off a sense of foreboding.

A voice said, 'Fleur, are you OK? That sure was one angry man in that car.'

She opened her eyes. 'Jake! Jake Merton, what . . . ?'

'I got your message. That was angry, too. What's going on?'

'I think I made that clear enough. The Manoir is not for sale, so you've had a wasted journey.'

Jake shook his head, his eyes puzzled.

'I've a busy morning if you don't mind.' Fleur turned to go, still angry and unsettled by her stepfather's visit. 'Please leave.'

Jake took a step towards her, put his hand on her shoulder. 'Listen, Fleur, I can . . .'

Angrily she shook his hand away. 'Don't. You can't flatter and fool me again. Just leave.'

'But I don't understand.'

'Just go away.' She could feel the tears behind her anger.

'Fleur, don't be like this. I can explain. Amanda . . .'

'No! Just go!'

Again he moved to touch her and she felt herself weakening. She wanted his touch, his comfort. 'I . . .' she faltered, then a cold voice cut the atmosphere.

'Fleur, Mrs Weston, is this man

bothering you?' Christopher Jones stepped on to the terrace.

Jake took a step back. 'I'm talking to Mrs Weston. And what's that got to do with you?'

'Mrs Weston has asked you to leave,' Christopher Jones said.

Jake frowned. 'Fleur, is this man a friend of yours?'

'No, he's a guest. And please go, Jake, I really don't want to talk to you. I've nothing more to say, except that the Manoir is NOT for sale.'

Jake looked from Fleur to Christopher Jones standing protectively beside her. 'But Fleur . . . '

'You heard Mrs Weston,' Christopher Jones said, 'you should go.'

'Fleur . . . ' One last appeal, but she turned away.

'Go, Jake,' she said quietly.

For some moments he stood looking at her, then with a small shake of his head, he left, got into his car, turned around on the gravel driveway and drove towards the gate.

★ ★ ★

For a few seconds Fleur stood silent, conflicting emotions hammering at her heart. She longed to call Jake back, but then she remembered, he was only after her estate. Hadn't his personal assistant told her that? All that talk about the spark between them . . .

'I'm sorry, Fleur, I didn't mean to interfere, but you looked so upset. I thought the young man was bothering you. Did I do wrong?' Mr Jones said anxiously.

Fleur shook her head. 'No. But I had another visitor, just before Jake. He was the one who really upset me. I'm afraid I was a bit hard on Jake. I didn't let him explain.'

'Is he really after your Manoir?'

'Oh, I don't know, I'm maybe losing my sense of proportion, becoming paranoid about it. First my stepfather, then some anonymous offer, then you, then Jake . . . '

'I think he looked a very genuine

young man. I just acted on instinct. I'm sorry if I've upset you.'

'You haven't, let's forget it. Are you staying much longer, Mr Jones?'

'I plan on a few more days. I have business in Paris but I'd like to stay here again on my way back to England.'

'Check with Aimee, she'll book you in. Now, if you'll excuse me, I should be in my office.'

'Of course.' His eyes followed her until she was out of sight, then he sat on the terrace for a long time, his eyes clouded with sad melancholy.

★ ★ ★

Fleur stared at the pile of paperwork on her desk. Mechanically, she checked on current and future bookings: August at the Manoir was full, September the same and October promising. She had every reason to be satisfied, even jubilant, that her venture was succeeding well beyond her expectations, yet her sense of unease persisted. Her encounters with her stepfather, Jake, and the mysterious Mr Jones had thoroughly unsettled her.

With an impatient shake of her head, she pulled a pile of invoices towards her and made herself concentrate on bringing her balance sheets up to date. It was unusually difficult to concentrate and her head began to ache.

Daisy burst into her office. 'Mum! Look, look! Baby 'matoes.'

'For goodness' sake, Daisy, do be quiet, I'm working,' Fleur snapped, with uncharacteristic impatience.

Daisy let out a squeal of dismayed hurt and threw herself on the floor.

'Oh, Daisy, Daisy, I'm sorry. Here, let me see, come on,' she knelt and picked up her daughter in an enveloping hug. 'Let me see.'

But Daisy was only partly mollified. She shook her head and closed her fist over her precious tomatoes.

'Come on, Daisy, I've said I'm sorry. I was busy, that's all. You don't like

165

being interrupted when you're busy, do you?'

'Mmm. OK you can see my 'matoes.' She held out two tiny fruits and popped one in her mouth and one in Fleur's.

The sweet burst of flavour took Fleur by surprise. 'Wow! Lovely.'

'I'll get more tomorrow,' Daisy said, and wriggled off Fleur's knee.

'But only if Georges allows,' Fleur warned.

'He will,' Daisy said, and was away to the vegetable garden, happy again.

★   ★   ★

Fleur closed her folders, shut her eyes and tried to relax the tension which had been building all day. She took deep breaths, rubbed her temples and slowly regained her composure. She'd follow Daisy to the vegetable garden — it was always a calming place.

As she passed Reception, Aimee beckoned, face wreathed in smiles, brandishing a fistful of euros. 'Fleur, look, a huge tip. The guy in the garden cottage just checked out. He apologises but he had urgent business. He enjoyed his stay and wishes you and Daisy good luck for the future.'

'Wow,' Fleur counted the euros, 'this is way over the top. I'll put it in the staff box. He was a bit strange, our Mr Jones, don't you think?'

Her mobile pre-empted a reply. It was Jane, just docking at Plymouth. 'Hi, Fleur. Thanks so much for the break. And I suddenly remembered where I've seen your mystery man. It was in London, at the flats. He was looking for Babette Remondin. Isn't that strange?'

A Disastrous Occurrence

Fleur and Tim were sipping a pre-breakfast coffee on the terrace in the early morning sunshine. Tim was keen to turn the chapel into a second holiday cottage. 'You could open it next season, I could get the plans drawn up,' he told Fleur.

'Hey, slow down, there's still this first season to get through.'

'But you're fully booked, things are going great and with a second holiday cottage you could do even better.'

'Finance, Tim, remember? I don't want to overstretch myself.'

Tim stirred his coffee. 'I could help with the finance.'

'Tim! I'd no idea you were rich!' Fleur grinned.

'I'm not, but my dad is, and he's

always looking for a good investment.'

Just then, a camper van came up the drive and Fleur jumped up. 'The family for the garden cottage. I must see to them.'

'OK, but think about my offer. And before you dash off, don't forget supper tonight with Celeste and me in town. I'll pick you up at six o'clock.'

'Tim, I couldn't possibly take an evening off.'

'Yes you can. It's all organised.'

'But . . . '

'No buts. See you tonight.'

⋆ ⋆ ⋆

'There's Celeste, over there,' Tim said, pointing to a table by the window.

'But she's not alone.'

'No, she's with an old friend, you'll like him.'

Fleur's heart sank. Please, not a blind date. She'd thought these embarrassing occasions were behind her. The girls as Simkins had tried a few times to pair her off with so-called eligible prospects: blind dates, surprise parties, even speed dating. She'd avoided most of them but occasionally she'd gone along with what was planned. It had never worked. They were all pleasant enough young men, but they just reminded her too much of what she'd lost in Ben. No-one ever matched up to him.

She looked reproachfully at Tim.

'He's in property,' Tim said hastily, 'he might be useful to you.'

Celeste kissed Fleur on both cheeks before introducing her to the young man. 'Antoine, one of my oldest friends. We were childhood sweet-hearts.'

Tall, good-looking, the man shook hands with Fleur. 'She's not joking, I was madly in love with Celeste when I was eleven. Hello, Fleur, I've heard a lot about you and your Manoir.'

Antoine turned out to be good company, and Fleur began to enjoy herself.

'I'd love to see your Manoir,' Antoine

said. 'I manage holiday lets and houses for British people working here. They often need stopovers before going South. Your Manoir sounds very suitable.'

'Come and visit and I'll give you some brochures.'

'And if you expand . . . ' Tim started eagerly.

'Tim, don't rush me. I need to be cautious at this stage. I told you.'

'Tim, you'll frighten Fleur off.' Celeste put her hand on Tim's arm. He took her hand and kissed it. 'All right, I'll come clean. I want to stay here, leave London, live in France permanently. I love living here and . . . ' He took both of Celeste's hands in his, 'more than anything I love Celeste . . . and a reason for inviting you, Fleur, and Antoine, both close friends of both of us, is to announce our engagement. I've asked Celeste to marry me, and she's said yes!'

'Wow!' Fleur hugged Celeste and kissed Tim. 'Wonderful, marvellous news! And you'll live here in Brittany, near the Manoir?'

'I doubt the Dubois family would allow me to marry Celeste if I planned to carry her off to London!'

'Ah, but we will visit England, lots. I'd love to meet your family, Tim, and yours, too, Fleur.'

'Well, you've met my family — myself and Daisy. That's all there is.'

News of the engagement filtered through the restaurant. Several customers knew Celeste and Antoine and a constant stream of congratulations turned the evening into a party, so when Fleur decided it was time to leave, she was horrified to see how late it was.

'Tim, Celeste, I must go. I'll get a taxi.'

'I must leave too,' Antoine said. 'Perhaps we could share the cab?'

'Fine, if the Manoir's in your direction.'

'Practically on the same route.'

Tim and Celeste looked set to stay

longer, enjoying their special moment.

'Congratulations both,' Fleur said as she put on her coat. 'I couldn't be happier for you.'

'You don't mind?' Tim said. 'And you can see why I'd like to put money into your Manoir?'

'I don't mind a bit, you should know that. And we'll talk about the Manoir later.'

★ ★ ★

The taxi driver stopped by the terrace. Antoine got out to open Fleur's door. 'Thanks,' she said, 'and I won't forget the brochures.'

'Could I phone you? Maybe a drink, supper?'

'I'm sorry, Antoine, right now I have to focus on the Manoir, but I've really enjoyed this evening. Maybe when the season's over, I'll be less busy.'

'OK, I'll keep you to that.' He kissed her lightly on the cheek before getting back into the taxi.

As she watched the cab drive away, a wave of sadness swept over Fleur. Such a nice guy, attractive, good company, but he wasn't Jake. She gasped. Jake, she'd thought, not Ben. For the first time she'd compared a man with someone other than Ben.

'Sorry, Ben,' she whispered, but strangely, she didn't feel any pangs of guilt. Time to move on? Isn't that what Ben would have wanted?

She turned towards the Manoir, opening her bag for keys. As she did so, her heart missed a beat. She hadn't noticed it before, but there was a light on in the chapel. Had a member of staff left it on? Oh, she was too tired to think about it now. But the following day, Fleur had something much more serious to deal with than the light left on in the chapel.

Just as dawn was breaking, Hortense, the Manoir housekeeper, knocked on her door. 'Come quickly, please, Fleur, there is a sick guest.'

'Oh, dear. Who is it? What's the

problem?' She pulled on her dressing-gown.

'Mrs Burton, from London. She's been here a week. She and her husband were leaving today, but I'm sure she's too ill to travel. Her husband's frantic.'

The Burtons' room was on the second floor. 'Mr Burton,' Fleur said as she knocked on the door. 'Can I come in?'

'Thank goodness.' A frantic-looking Mr Burton opened the door. 'My wife's been ill all night.'

The Burtons, sprightly sixty-year-olds, had had a week of walking the coast paths, both looking the picture of fitness. Now, Mrs Burton, drained of colour, lifted a feeble hand to Fleur, 'Sorry dear, I can't think what's happened. I can't even keep a drink of water down.'

'When did it start, Mrs Burton?' Fleur took her hand and felt her forehead.

'After supper last night, don't ask me what we ate, the very thought of food . . . ' She groaned.

'All right, don't worry, I'll call the doctor.'

'I'm so sorry to be a nuisance.'

'Nonsense. Now you must rest. Mr Burton, are you OK?'

'I think so, just a bit queasy. Sympathy symptoms maybe . . .' But his face was drained of its normal healthy colour.

'I'll phone the doctor immediately,' Fleur said. 'Hortense, can you stay with Mr and Mrs Burton in case they need anything.'

It was too early for the local surgery, but Fleur had an emergency number. She described the Burtons' symptoms. 'I can't imagine they'll be fit to travel today, they both look dreadful. Oh, and Mrs Burton's a diabetic, would that be a factor?'

'Only if she's badly dehydrated. I'll come up right away. Mrs Weston, isn't it?' the doctor said. 'My wife and I had supper at the Manoir just last week, quite delightful, you've a great chef. Polish?'

'Stefan, yes. You don't think . . . our food . . . ?'

'Could be anything. Did the sick guests eat in the restaurant?'

'Very probably, they love the food there. I'll check.'

'Good. Don't worry too much, these things happen. Check the status of your other guests, discreetly, of course. And don't worry, Mrs Weston, I'm sure it will prove to be a one-off. I'll be with you shortly.'

Fleur dressed, checked on Daisy who was sound asleep, then hurried down to the kitchen where Stefan and his new Polish assistant had already started breakfast.

'Hi, Fleur, what's up?'

'There's a problem.' Quickly she explained about the Burtons.

'Did they have supper here last night?' she asked, but already she knew the answer. The Burtons ate at the Manoir every night, always praising Stefan's food.

'Yes, they did and they enjoyed it, so

they said. This is terrible, Fleur, but I am one hundred percent certain that whatever it is, this illness did not come from my kitchen.'

'What did they eat, can you remember?'

'Sure — zupa koperkowa, dill soup — then bouillibaise, a mix of Polish and French. They ate the same thing every night.'

'Was the fish from the new supplier?'

'Yes. We checked it over last night, together, remember, just before Tim came for you.'

'The new fish supplier, he's reliable?'

'Absolutely. Local man and his son selling from their own boat. There's nothing in this kitchen that could cause illness. You do believe me, don't you, Fleur?'

'Of course I do.'

Fleur looked at the shining stainless steel surfaces, gleaming pan racks, and spotless ovens. 'But we might get inspected anyway — just routine.' Look, you carry on with the breakfasts, but any sign of illness among the guests, let me know at once.'

'Of course, Fleur. And don't look so worried. It'll be fine.'

'I hope you're right.'

On her way back to her office, Fleur looked in on the dining room. She hung around for a while, greeting her guests. The majority looked fit and healthy, with a few a bit glum because it was the end of their holiday. Only one elderly gentleman on his own at a window table was looking at his food rather than eating it. Fleur slid into the empty seat opposite him. 'Mr Moon, you're not eating much, don't you feel well?'

He patted his stomach and winced. 'Usual trouble, Mrs Weston, over-eating, food's too good here. You see, I live on my own, don't cook much, so when I can get such wonderful food as the Manoir provides I over-indulge.' He smiled at her. 'I have enjoyed it thoroughly, though. I'm leaving today but I've booked in for a week in the autumn. You've done a good job here, young lady. I wish you well.'

'Thank you.' Fleur could have kissed him. Maybe she was worrying about nothing. After all, people did get ill on holiday.

Feeling more cheerful, she went upstairs to the Burtons' room and met the doctor coming downstairs.

'Ah, Mrs Weston, I assume.' He held out his hand. 'Phillipe Laval.'

'Thank you for coming so promptly, doctor. What do you think is wrong with the Burtons?'

'I'm not sure, but as a precaution I'm admitting them to hospital. Mrs Burton is severely dehydrated and as she's a diabetic we need to get fluids into her. Mr Burton's not too bad, but he might as well go with her. I'll keep you in the picture. The ambulance will be along any minute.'

'Ambulance! Oh dear.'

'Just a precaution,' the doctor said, 'and do let me know at once if anyone else is poorly. Oh, and you may get a visit from Health and Hygiene. Just routine.'

It was Fleur's worst nightmare, two guests carried out on stretchers by paramedics and an ambulance flashing its lights in the drive as if to advertise the calamity.

Mr Burton looked apologetically up at Fleur. 'So sorry, my dear, terrible publicity for you.'

Fleur hadn't actually thought about the publicity angle, though now she was aware of other guests coming out of the breakfast room, gathering in the entrance hall.

'Whatever's going on?'

'Who is it?'

'Couple from London . . . nice pair . . . look terrible.'

'Something they ate . . . ?'

As the ambulance drew away, the guests gathered around Fleur.

'What is it?'

'Serious?'

'Something they ate?'

A silence fell as the guests tried to

remember what they'd eaten for supper and whether they suddenly felt a bit off-colour.

'Please,' Fleur said soothingly, 'I'll let you know as soon as I know. Some of you are leaving this afternoon and I'll give you any news I hear from the hospital before you go. I'm sorry if this should spoil your last day here.'

* * *

Fleur went upstairs to the Burton's room. Hortense was stripping the beds and there was a strong smell of disinfectant. Fleur opened the window. 'They may be coming back, Hortense. We shall have to keep their room, their things are still here.'

Hortense looked out of the front-facing windows. 'There's a car coming up the drive, it can't get past the ambulance. A man's getting out, looking cross, arms waving. Oh dear, he's having to reverse and go the other way round.'

'Thanks. I'll go down and sort it out.'

In the main reception area, Aimee's look of relief when Fleur appeared was a sure sign something was wrong. 'Oh Fleur, I'm so glad you're here. I've booked the Parker family in and they've gone to their rooms, but Mr and Mrs Browne here aren't at all happy. They're waiting to speak to you' She indicated a middle-aged couple.

'You the owner of this place?' the man said curtly.

'I am Fleur Weston. Can I help?'

'You can begin by explaining why your drive was blocked by an ambulance carrying out two of your guests with food poisoning. A very good start to our holiday, I don't think. We have to eat out, I assume.'

'Of course not, and it's not at all certain it is food poisoning.'

'That's what everyone is saying. But be that as it may, we've examined the room where we're supposed to be accommodated. Far too dark and no television. It's not good enough, Mrs Weston.'

Fleur summoned up her most charming smile. 'I'm so sorry if you don't like your room, Mr Browne. I can perhaps offer an alternative, though we are quite heavily booked.'

'I'm afraid that's not satisfactory. My wife is very upset; she has a delicate stomach and already feels ill at the thought of staying in a germ-laden atmosphere. We shall leave as soon as you have refunded our deposit, plus compensation for the inconvenience, of course.'

Fleur could have held claimed full payment from them, since there were no reasonable grounds for cancelling their booking, but she decided it wasn't worth the fuss. The man was thoroughly unpleasant and she would be well rid of him.

'I'll gladly refund your deposit,' she said, 'but as to compensation, I'm afraid I can't see sufficient grounds, Mr Browne. The Manoir is as advertised in our brochure.

'As to the food poisoning, that has

not been proved, and no-one else has been taken ill.' As she spoke, Fleur was writing a cheque, which she handed over. 'Here's your deposit. I hope you find something in the area more to your liking.'

'This isn't the end of the matter. You'll be hearing from my lawyer. Come along, Dorothy,' and Mr Browne stormed off, his wife meekly following.

'Goodness,' Aimee said, 'what a horrid man. We're well shot of him. I just pity the hotel he does decide to stay in.'

'I hope he wasn't rude to you, Aimee.'

Aimee shrugged. 'Doesn't bother me, it's one of the downsides of the job.'

'Aimee, can I leave you to cope here while I go to the kitchen?' Fleur asked.

'Of course.'

'Give me a call if there's another Mr Browne.'

'Statistically unlikely,' Aimee replied cheerfully.

In the kitchen, Fleur was assailed by a babble of furious Polish. Wanda was there, released from nanny duties by Daisy's three mornings a week's attendance at a local playgroup run by Celeste's aunt.

'What's the problem?' Fleur shouted above the clamour.

Wanda gestured to a kitchen helper. 'Stanislaus thinks we should close tonight just in case — Stefan disagrees.'

Fleur said, 'If we close, it would look as though we thought we were to blame for the Burtons' illness.'

'Exactly,' Stefan agreed. 'My kitchen is spotless, blameless. I invite anyone in to inspect it, day or night.'

'I'm sure you'll be in the clear, Stefan, but you know how rumours spread.'

'So I'll open tonight as usual?' Stefan turned to his assistant and Polish broke out once again.

*　★　★

'By the way, did the noise last night disturb you?' Wanda asked Fleur.

186

'No. What noise?'

Wanda laughed. 'Three lads went into town for a party and cheerfully admitted they'd overdone their celebrations. Stefan heard them stumbling around, trying to get in the chapel instead of the house.'

'Oh really? That could explain it, then. When I got back last night, I thought there was a light on in the chapel.'

'Oh, they didn't get in, just banged about a bit.'

'Still, I expect that does explain it.'

* * *

By mid-morning the Manoir was quiet. New arrivals had been settled in and were already out exploring the area. All expressed satisfaction with their accommodation.

Fleur was about to settle down to some paperwork when she remembered the chapel. Although reassured by Wanda's explanation, she decided to take a look anyway.

She walked around the Manoir, enjoying the clear, golden sunshine. There had been no rain to speak of for weeks and although visitors loved it, Georges was in despair at the amount of watering his vegetable garden needed.

The chapel, mellow in the sunshine, looked peaceful and inviting. Fleur stood outside for a few minutes imagining the Remondin family, her ancestors, assembling here for morning prayers. Maybe a Remondin was married here, even buried somewhere. She thought of Yvette, the young bride in the copse. Why was she not in the chapel or her local church?

She unlocked the heavy wooden door and went inside. Here the light was softer, only shafts of sunlight from the high stained glass windows allowed muted sunshine. The main room had been cleared, with just a few boxes and paint cans left. Two doors behind the small pulpit led to underground rooms and passages. Fleur tried both doors. Locked. She had no idea where the keys were or even what was behind the doors. Pierre Dubois had spoken of underground cellars, but there had been no time to explore in the race to get the main house ready for the season.

She went closer to one of the locked doors. The floor was dusty with cement and there were footmarks, right by the door. They looked newly-made. She bent down to examine them — men's shoes or boots, maybe, left over from Pierre's builders. But she was certain Pierre had swept the place clean. Then she remembered Tim, he was interested in converting the chapel to a holiday home. He must have been in here.

She was somehow relieved to know there was a simple explanation.

Fleur Is Angry

When Fleur arrived back to the Manoir, Aimee met her at the door, holding out the phone. 'Dr Laval, from the hospital.'

Fleur took the phone and crossed her fingers.

'Mrs Weston, you can stop worrying. The Burtons suffered an allergic reaction, admittedly in your restaurant, but certainly nothing to do with your kitchen. Just an unfortunate circumstance. Mr Burton does recall a fish he'd never heard of in your chef's bouillibaise. You'd better warn him to check with his supplier. But you and your Manoir are blameless.'

'Thank goodness for that. Strange it was just the Burtons, though.'

'Maybe it was their age, and of

course, Mrs Burton is a diabetic. Anyway, both of them are comfortable and with good luck should be back with you tomorrow at the earliest.'

'I'm very grateful, Dr Laval, and we'll be very pleased to see you at our restaurant, a meal for two on the house.'

'That's very kind. My wife will be pleased. But I think we'll avoid the bouillibaise!'

Greatly relieved, Fleur went to tell Stefan the good news. 'Fleur, I am so sorry. The bouillibaise is so popular with the customers.'

'No need to abandon it, just stick to the tried and tested fish.'

'Ah well,' he sighed, 'but I do love experimenting, which reminds me, there's something I'd like to discuss with you.'

'Sure. I've a minute right now.'

'OK,' Stefan took a deep breath, 'I'd like to run a cookery school here at the Manoir, obviously mainly in the winter. I could maybe start in the chapel, then later, if it's a success, the stable block could convert to kitchens and accommodation for pupils.'

Fleur was impressed by Stefan's ambition, but a bit taken aback. 'Let me think about it, Stefan. The conversions would cost a bomb. And, what about Wanda? Wouldn't a cookery school here tie you to Brittany?'

'Of course, but we both love it here, and Wanda is becoming more interested it the restaurant trade. Daisy is growing up so quickly, too. Wanda is beginning to feel she may soon be surplus to requirements.'

'Oh, no! I can't do without Wanda, not yet.'

'You won't have to. Daisy and you are Wanda's first priority, but by the time we had a cookery school up and running, Daisy would be nearly school age.'

'I suppose,' Fleur said, and frowned.

'Not such a good idea then, the cookery school?' Stefan looked disappointed.

'No, no, it's not that. It's just Daisy growing up so fast . . .' And always the sad, inevitable thought, Daisy growing up without a father. Without Ben.

'Fleur,' Stefan looked worried, 'have I upset you?'

'No, of course not, it's just that sometimes I feel . . . '

'Fleur, you are a very capable woman, but on your own it must be hard, maybe one day . . . ' He stopped, it wasn't his place to say what both he and Wanda felt, that one day, Fleur would meet someone who would love her and Daisy. 'Forget my cookery school nonsense,' he said, 'it's much too early. But I'll just say for now that money wouldn't be a problem. My father in Poland is a wealthy man, he made much money out of salt and he wants to invest in me.'

'Salt! Well, that's a change from property! I am interested in your idea, Stefan, but let's get a little more established with what we've got at present. And just pray there aren't any more setbacks like today.'

'Oh no, we have had our share of mishaps for now,' Stefan said confidently.

★ ★ ★

At first it seemed Stefan's optimism was justified. The Manoir was fully booked, the Burtons recovered and fortunately the garden cottage was free for a couple of days and the couple spent a peaceful recuperation there at Fleur's expense, though they them-selves were eager to pay her.

It was the day after the Burtons left the Manoir that the next bombshell burst: Fleur was in her office, Wanda had taken Daisy to playgroup but returned white-faced with the local paper. 'Fleur, this is awful. How dare he? It's lies, lies and more lies.'

'What? What is it?'

Wanda opened the newspaper at the centre pages. 'Look. There are pictures, and everything.'

Fleur read the thick black headline:

'Ill-fated Manoir de Belvoir.' The main picture was of the Manoir and underneath were two smaller photographs, one of the chapel and one of . . . Fleur gasped . . . Yvette's grave!

Fleur read with growing anger and disbelief:

'*Manoir de Belvoir, beautiful view maybe, but ill-luck continues to follow the unfortunate Remondins. New owner Fleur Weston, daughter of the late Babette Remondin, has brought disaster with her from the United Kingdom. Older readers will recall the Remondin misfortunes of the war years. The male Remondins killed in World War One. The sad young bride buried in the grounds. The last of the male Remondins killed during World War Two. And misfortune still dogs the Remondin heels. Only recently an outbreak of food poisoning from the Manoir kitchens nearly closed down the establishment. It remains to be seen whether Fleur Weston can turn the curse of the Remondins into a profitable business. We think it very doubtful.*'

Furious, Fleur telephoned the local paper and was put through to the editor. 'André Bonet,' a youngish voice said.

Fleur took a deep breath. 'M. Bonet, I have just read your scurrilous, totally incorrect article on the Manoir de Belvoir. It is quite outrageous and I want an immediate retraction and apology.'

'Er . . . Mrs Weston?'

'Yes, of course it's Mrs Weston. And I must inform you that you have strung together a piece full of inaccuracies. We did not have an outbreak of food poisoning. A couple of guests had an allergic reaction to some fish, no-one else was affected. And as far as the Remondin ill luck, and some sort of curse on the Manoir, that is fanciful conjecture.

'Your article is a spiteful and wicked piece of journalism and I want it retracted immediately on the front

196

page, otherwise my lawyer will be contacting you.'

There was a long silence at the other end of the phone. 'M. Bonet, are you still there?' Fleur asked.

'Yes, sorry, Mrs Weston. Look, could we meet? Maybe I could come out to the Manoir.'

'That's probably a very good idea. Perhaps you could inspect our kitchens while you're at it!'

'All right, Mrs Weston. Tomorrow suit you?'

'Today would be better.'

'Today, then. In fact, I'll come right now.'

'Oh, fine.'

* * *

Unable to settle to work, she went into the kitchen where Stefan was reading the article. 'Crazy,' he said when she arrived. 'Apart from the food poisoning lie, what's all this about the Remondins?'

'The bare bones are true if Georges' great-grandfather is anything to go by, and the Remondin fortunes have certainly declined over the years. Do you think it'll put people off?' Fleur asked anxiously.

'We've had a couple of cancellations, though they did say it was illness in the family. I'd like to get my hands on this editor. Did he write the piece himself?'

'I don't imagine so, but Stefan, I'm worried. It's a strange article, and there is a bit of truth in it about the Remondins. Someone's been digging around. And why make mention of Yvette's grave?'

'No idea. But it's only a local rag. The majority of our customers come from the UK. They'll never see this.'

'I hope you're right.'

* * *

M. Bonet was ushered into Fleur's office by a stern-looking Aimee. 'Thanks, Aimee. We'll go into the garden room, I think that's free at the moment. Would you be so kind, Aimee — some coffee?'

'Right away.'

'Follow me, M. Bonet.' Fleur, showing off her Manoir, deliberately led the editor through the hall into the lounge with its conservatory extension. Sunlight streamed into the room. 'Please sit down, M. Bonet, and tell me why you chose to libel my Manoir and, what is worse, my family.'

'I'm sorry,' M. Bonet replied bluntly, 'but I didn't have a say in the matter. I'm fairly new as editor, still finding my feet. The paper's owner is a local businessman and the article was written by a friend of his. I don't want this repeated, Mrs Weston, but I think my owner was paid to print the article.'

'Paid? Why should anyone pay to libel my business?'

'No idea, but you see, I won't be able to print a retraction. I'm sorry, especially as I can see this would be a lovely place to stay.'

Aimee appeared with the coffee.

'Thanks, Aimee,' Fleur smiled. 'Everything OK?'

Aimee looked meaningfully at M. Bonet. 'A couple more restaurant bookings just cancelled. Said they were ill — didn't sound like it to me.' She glared at M. Bonet, who shuffled his feet and gulped his coffee. 'I'm sorry, I will talk to my proprieter, tell him I've been here, seen the house . . . ' He put his cup down. 'Would you know why anyone would want to discredit you? A business rival, perhaps, a dissatisfied customer?'

'We don't have those,' Aimee spoke sharply. 'Ah!' She looked at Fleur. 'Remember the angry man who didn't like his room?'

'Mr Browne? Surely not. What would be the point?' Fleur frowned. 'And all that about the Remondin family and the grave, he wouldn't know about that.'

'Mrs Weston, I honestly shouldn't worry too much. I hate to admit it, but our circulation is pretty small, more a local advertiser than a newspaper.'

'I hope you're right, M. Bonet, but even so, I should like you to talk to your owner, better still, ask him to talk to me, come himself to take a look at the Manoir.'

'I'll do what I can.' M. Bonet sighed. 'I think it's time I moved on anyway. Maybe to Paris.'

'I wish you luck. Now, would you like to take a look at our kitchen and restaurant?'

After the kitchen visit, Fleur heard no more from M. Bonet and when she telephoned the *Advertiser* a few days later, she was told he had left to work in Paris.

She tried to forget the article, and for the next few days, things returned to something like normal. There were one or two more cancellations and Stefan's restaurant wasn't quite so busy, but it was late August and most of the locals were still away on their own holidays, so the restaurant had to rely more on the tourist trade. Fleur began to hope the article was a one-day wonder and unlikely to be read in the wider world. That was, until Tim came up to the Manoir the following Sunday morning.

'Fleur,' he waved a newspaper at her, 'that article — it's in the travel sections of the Sunday papers, French and British, and it's longer, with pictures. It's a main feature.'

Fleur's heart sank as she flipped over the pages. There were glossy photos of the Manoir before and after the renovation and, inevitably, a picture of Yvette's grave with the headstone and inscription.

'Oh Tim,' Fleur said wearily, 'it's a campaign. Someone, and there are plenty of suspects, wants me out of here.'

'Who?'

'I wouldn't put it past my stepfather. Then there's that wealthy-looking bloke, Christopher Jones. Then there's Celeste's original buyer.'

'No, no, not them, that was just a tentative enquiry, a likely-looking investment. Celeste can vouch for them.'

'And then,' Fleur said slowly, 'there's Jake Merton.'

'Jake? The American? Come on, Fleur, he's not interested in the Manoir. It's you he's interested in, and I thought you felt the same way about him. No, I guarantee Jake Merton has no interest in the Manoir de Belvoir, only its proprietor.'

'Well why isn't he here, then?' Fleur burst out.

'Didn't you send him away with a flea in his ear? Hey,' he went over to the window, 'what the heck? I don't believe it, a group of people with cameras are going towards the copse. Come on, Fleur.'

Just then the phone rang and Daisy ran into the room. 'Tim,' she cried out and jumped into his arms. 'Tim — come see my 'matoes. I've saved you some.'

'Daisy, that's great, but right now I have to go outside.'

'I'll come with you,' Daisy said, and took Tim's hand.

'Go on,' Fleur said. 'I'll get the phone.'

As Tom and Daisy left, Fleur picked up the phone.

'Fleur?'

Her heart flipped. It was unmistakable, the deep male voice with more than a trace of an American accent.

'It's Jake. I've just seen the Sunday supplement travel section. What the heck is all that about?'

Her heart resumed its normal rhythm. 'Oh, just a bit of adverse publicity.'

'Look, I'm in London just now but I'm on my way to Brittany.'

'Why? Because of a newspaper article?'

'Fleur, please, I was on my way to see you anyway. My flight was booked days ago, before I even set eyes on this article.'

'Oh.' Fleur held the phone tightly.

'Fleur, I must see you, the last weeks have been dreadful. I'll explain when I see you. I've got to go now; I'm having supper with Jane and Sam. They send their love. Bye for now, Fleur.'

Fleur shivered, closed her eyes and let herself visualise Jake. It was easy; she could remember every detail of his voice, his smile, his kiss.

Tim and Daisy came back into the office, but Fleur hardly heard them.

'Hey, Fleur, what's up? I thought you were following us. Are you OK? Not bad news?' Tim said.

'No, not bad news.' Fleur swept Daisy into her arms.

'Hey, Mum, 'matoes all squashed.' Aggrieved, Daisy held out a couple of squashed tomatoes.

'Sorry, love. Never mind, we can still eat them.'

'It's not the point,' Daisy said severely. 'There's only a few left and Georges told off the people, didn't he, Tim?'

'He did, in no uncertain terms,' Tim agreed.

'What people did Georges tell off, and what for? He's not upsetting the guests, I hope,' Fleur said.

'Fleur. Those guys wandering in the grounds, they wanted to see the grave, take pictures.'

'But whatever for?'

'No idea, but they seemed genuinely interested in Yvette's story. You know, Fleur, this may backfire on whoever's behind this. Was that a customer on the phone already?'

'Actually it was Jake Merton. He's coming over.'

'Ah ha! Told you so, didn't I?'

'It still may be the property he's interested in.'

'Oh, Fleur, the poor guy is interested in you, not the Manoir. You will see him, won't you?'

'Yes, it would be rude not to.'

'Of course it would,' Tim grinned.

'Jake?' Daisy looked up from trying to de-squash her tomatoes. 'Jake's nice, almost as nice as Tim.'

'Well, thank you, Daisy, a compliment to be sure, but Jake's just as nice as me.'

Jake Merton Returns

Fleur telephoned the editor of the Sunday newspaper that had carried the article about the Manoir and the Remondins.

He was charming but firm. 'Sorry, Mrs Weston, I can't divulge our source, except to say it was passed on by your local newspaper.'

'But wouldn't you check the facts of such a condemning article, or at least contact me as the owner of the Manoir? I'm bound to lose business, I've already had a couple of cancellations.'

'That's a shame, but you know the saying, no such thing as bad publicity. I believe you'll benefit in the long run. The young bride buried in the grounds, that's sure to be a draw.'

'I do hope not! Why would anyone

want to visit the grave of someone they don't know?'

'You'd be surprised. It's romantic and sad, and there's the family history too, very intriguing.'

'If you say so, but at least you should retract the bit about food poisoning, that's very damaging. My two guests suffered an allergic reaction and I have medical proof of that.'

'I'll be happy to do that.'

'And you can't, or won't, tell me who wrote the article?'

'Sorry, I can't give you the name. Truly though, he or she has probably done you a favour. Wait and see, you'll have people on your doorstep looking for the grave, trying out your restaurant. You're on the map, Mrs Weston.'

And to Fleur's astonishment, the editor proved to be correct. There were few cancellations, and the locals knew Stefan's cooking was excellent and continued to patronise the restaurant.

But the slur rankled in Fleur's mind.

Someone was trying to damage her reputation. That, combined with her stepfather's continuous insistence that he had a claim on the Manoir, and the mysterious Christopher Jones, continued to worry her. She couldn't even be sure about Jake.

But there was one local who had already benefited from the article.

* * *

Fleur and Daisy were in the vegetable garden picking the last of Daisy's tomatoes when a group of people appeared in the grounds. Fleur didn't recognise any of them and they were certainly not guests from the Manoir. Seeing her, one of the group gave her a cheery wave before disappearing towards the copse.

'Georges,' Fleur frowned, 'friends of yours?'

'Not exactly, but . . . oh dear, I'd better come clean. You know we've had the odd tourist wanting to see the grave of the young Remondin wife? I chased them off at first, as you know, but one day my great-grandad had wandered over. You said it was all right for him to sit out there while I'm working.'

'Yes, of course, I've met him, he's a dear, but . . . '

'A couple of people were looking at the grave, reading the inscription, and old Henri got chatting to them about the Remondins and how he used to work here as a boy. They lapped it up and people began to come just to hear his tales of the past.'

'Really? And there are actually people wanting to look at the grave?'

'Seems so. There's a back entrance from the main road which leads directly to the copse. There is a gate, but it's easy to climb over.'

'Is Henri there now?'

'Henri's fun,' Daisy had been listening and chimed in, 'tells me stories.'

'A couple of times when Daisy was tending her tomatoes and radishes, she and Grandad have had a chat.' Georges leaned on his hoe. 'I can stop him coming any time, Mrs Weston and I'll get rid of the tourists.'

Fleur thought for a minute. While she certainly didn't want poor Yvette's grave to become a tourist attraction, she couldn't really see any harm in it. Interest would soon die down and if it gave the old man some pleasure in the meantime, what was the harm? 'No, don't stop your great-grandad coming,' she told Georges. 'It's extraordinary what interests people, but I can't imagine why anyone would want to visit the grave of a perfect stranger.'

'Well, I suppose it's kind of sad and romantic. And it is a bit unusual to lay your wife to rest in the garden.'

'Just what the editor of the Sunday paper said.'

'No more 'matoes.' Daisy had picked the last of her special plants and looked fit to cry.

Georges knelt down. 'Don't fret, Daisy. You know what, when I've time,

211

I'm going to mark you out a little garden of your very own and we'll work it together. Next year you can grow strawberries, salads and more tomatoes. Would you like that?'

'Oh, yes, yes. Please, Mum?'

'Of course, that'd be lovely. Thanks, Georges. But now, Daisy, we must go in and take your last tomatoes to Stefan to put in his special salads.'

'Can't I have one?' Daisy pleaded.

'I expect he'll spare you a couple, then Wanda will be wanting to start your bath and I have to change to see to my customers before dinner. Come and help me choose a pretty dress.'

On a fine evening, guests had drinks served on the terrace. After that, Fleur took over Daisy's bedtime while Wanda went down to help Stefan in the restaurant. It worked well and Fleur was delighted Wanda and Stefan had plans to stay on at the Manoir.

Fleur was pleased the way things were working out. The only cloud on the horizon was Paul Maynard. He had not

visited for a week or so, but he bom-
barded her with letters, still demanding
a share in the Manoir.

* * *

'This one,' Daisy pointed to a pair of
black silk trousers and a filmy white
top. 'This is pretty.'

'OK, that's it then, it should be warm
enough. Shoes?'

Daisy picked out a pair of soft leather
white sandals with a silver trim.

'What a useful girl you are, Daisy.'
Fleur quickly changed and brushed out
her dark hair.

'Hey, you look very smart.' Wanda
came into the room. 'Time for cocktails?'

Fleur pulled a face. 'I'd rather stay
here with Daisy, but I shan't be long.
It's hard work being polite and
charming when your mind's on other
things.'

* * *

Fleur went downstairs and out on to the terrace where the guests were already enjoying their drinks. She moved among them, advising on places to visit, making sure everyone was satisfied with their rooms. For a second she thought she glimpsed Christopher Jones, the mystery man, then someone asked about car hire, and when she looked again, he had disappeared.

Gradually, all the guests wandered towards the restaurant, leaving Fleur to savour the dying of the late summer evening. The blue sky was fading into a soft grey and pink sunset, day birds were hushed, night birds still waiting to emerge. It should have been a calming and peaceful moment, but Fleur felt strangely apprehensive. But she must be positive. She loved the Manoir, and it was going well. She had done, was doing, the right thing.

Optimism returning, she started to walk back towards the house. She'd reached the door to the Manoir when the sound of a car coming up the drive made her turn.

The car scrunched to a stop and a familiar figure leapt out and came towards her.

'Fleur.' Jake took her hands in his, and lightly kissed her cheek. 'Just where I left you,' he murmured. 'But I hope you're not as angry.'

'I . . . I was upset after my stepfather's visit and I thought you were after my Manoir, too.'

'And you wouldn't let me explain.' He stood back. 'You look lovely, Fleur.' He touched her hair, his hand lingering on her cheek, his dark blue eyes examining her intently. 'I've missed you. I should never have left you.'

'I'm sorry,' Fleur said. 'But at the time . . . '

He put his finger on her lips. 'Don't, Fleur. Concentrate on now. I've brought something to show you, but we need to go indoors. Where's Daisy?'

'Daisy's in bed. She'll be waiting for

her bedtime story. I was just going in to her.'

He took her hand. 'Then let's go say hello to her.'

Fleur clasped his hand in hers and felt a surge of joy. It was as natural as the starry sky to walk into the Manoir holding hands with Jake.

★ ★ ★

They had to pass through Reception to get to Fleur's apartment. Aimee looked up, and her eyes widened. 'It's Jake Merton, isn't it? Good to see you. Are you staying at the Manoir?'

'I'm afraid it'll be a bit difficult,' Fleur said. 'I don't think we've a room free until next week, have we, Aimee?'

'That's OK,' Jake said, 'I'm booked into a hotel in Morlaix. I had some business to attend to before I came down here, but I hope to persuade Fleur to spend the day with me tomorrow.'

'Oh, I can't . . . ' Fleur started, but Jake put his arm round her shoulders.

'You must, Fleur, Have you had any time off since you arrived at the Manoir?'

'No, she hasn't,' Aimee put in.

'But tomorrow's busy,' Fleur protested.

'Don't you trust your staff?' Aimee said.

'Of course I do,'

'Then prove it by taking tomorrow off.'

'Well . . . I do need to do some shopping.'

'Shopping!' Jake's tone was horrified. 'I was thinking of something much more exciting than shopping!'

'Well, all right then,' Fleur said. 'Now let's go up and see Daisy.' She noticed Jake was carrying a briefcase. 'Looks like you've come to work.'

'No, I haven't. This is the something I need to show you.'

* * *

Daisy and Wanda were cuddled up together on Daisy's bed, halfway through a story. For a moment Daisy looked puzzled, then her eyes lit up. 'The man in the swimming pool. Hello. I'm having my own garden, Georges says.'

'That'll be fun.' Jake sat on the end of Daisy's bed. 'I like gardening, at home we have a big garden.'

'Where's that?'

'America, a long way away.'

Daisy yawned and snuggled closer to Wanda. 'You finish my story, please.'

'Wanda has to go and help Stefan, pet,' Fleur said.

Daisy's eyelids drooped and Wanda gently disengaged herself from the bed. 'OK, see you later.'

Fleur kissed Daisy goodnight and tucked her in, and then she and Jake went into the sitting room. 'A bit basic, I'm afraid,' she apologised. 'I haven't got round to doing much to it. I'll get some coffee.'

'Wait a minute, Fleur, sit down.'

Jake opened his briefcase, pulled out a laptop and set it up on the coffee table. 'Fleur, you sent me away last time before I could explain. You wouldn't listen to me then. Will you now?'

She nodded, intrigued by the images on the laptop screen. 'What a beautiful house, it's huge, and the gardens . . . ' She watched, fascinated, as pictures of swimming pools, gyms, treatment rooms, lecture rooms, luxurious bedrooms, flicked across the screen. 'It's splendid, Jake. Is it some sort of spa?'

Jake nodded. 'The family business, Merton Inc., started by my great-grandfather. He was a doctor and an early pioneer of what were called health farms in those days. Pretty strict places, too. You can see how things have changed.'

'Extreme luxury living, judging by the pictures. It all looks wonderful, but why are you showing it to me?'

'Because, Fleur, I'm proving we're in totally different markets, and that I have no designs at all on your Manoir.'

'But your personal assistant, Amanda, told me you were looking for European outlets. Potential development, she said.'

'We are looking at Europe, but all our spas need to be right away from civilisation, and the Manoir is a little too near the town.' Jake laughed. 'Too many temptations for our clients. So can you believe me when I said I wasn't in the business of buying you out?'

Fleur felt a huge wave of relief, but a niggling doubt was still there. 'Why did you come to the Manoir, then? That couldn't have been coincidence.'

'Of course it wasn't. You must know, Fleur, that when we met on the stairs in London, there was a spark between us, electric, head-spinning.'

'But how did you know about the Manoir?' Fleur persisted.

'Jane, of course. I dragged out every bit of information from her that I could. I found out where you worked, about your family, Daisy, losing Ben, how much you loved him. Jane was reluctant at first but I persevered, and finally she told me about the Manoir and your plans. Then I simply followed your tracks and once I found you, I hated leaving, but I had to respect what you felt. Let's start over, Fleur. Please.'

Fleur was silent, watching him, testing her feelings, getting used to what he was saying. The luxury spas continued their slide show and Jake clicked off the computer and closed the laptop.

'I see the Manoir as a very poor relation to your spas, though it can be a healing place,' Fleur said at last.

'It is a very tranquil, calming place. At Merton we have more . . . austere places, but they do the same thing without the trappings. We can help people who can't afford the luxury trimmings.'

'And where do you fit in, Jake?'

'That's my side of the business. I've a medical degree, in psychiatry. I don't really fit in with the glamour image. I leave that to my father, two sisters and elder brother.'

'You've a big family?'

'Yes, quite an extended one.'

'Lucky you.'

'You're alone?'

'As Jane told you, completely, apart from my lovely Daisy, of course. Ben and I . . . well, we meant to have a large family. He was an only child, too.'

'I'm sorry, it must have been hard.'

'It still is sometimes. But I don't know what to say about your company, Merton.'

'Say nothing, just agree to have a drink with me.'

She nodded happily and he took her hand.

Together they went downstairs, only to be met by a tremendous commotion of adult voices and children's sobs.

'Oh no! Not more trouble,' Fleur said.

A Declaration Of Love

From the clamour, Fleur was expecting to find the full complement of the Manoir's guests in Reception. In fact, there were only two English families, who were holidaying together. Four adults were trying to calm down two hysterical little girls. Two older boys, obviously trying not to be noticed, were looking sheepish. 'Didn't mean any harm, Dad,' one of them said.

'Such a stupid thing to do, Jack,' said a distraught woman, who was trying to calm a frightened little girl.

'What's the matter, Mrs Walters?' Fleur asked.

'It's that grave, in your garden. It's frightened my Sophie.'

Jake joined the group and spoke to the little girl. 'What frightened you,

Sophie, and why were you out in the dark? The copse is a long way from the house.'

'It . . . ' she gulped down a sob, 'Jack said it was a dare, so . . . ' more sobs, 'Jenny and I got out of bed and went out. We didn't know it would be so dark.' She started to cry again and her father put his arm round her. 'Don't cry. Just tell us.'

'We went along the path, through the woody bit to the . . . the copse. The moon came out, we could see the clearing . . . '

'She was there!' the other little girl cried.

'Who was? What did you see?' Jake knelt to be on her level.

Sophie looked from brother, Jack, to her mother. 'Jack said he'd seen it last night. He said it was the lady's ghost. The one that's buried in the grave.'

'You idiot, Jack,' his father said.

'I didn't mean any harm, and we, Bill and me, followed them to make sure they were OK.'

'And did you see anything last night?' Jake asked.

'No. It was only a joke.'

'Not a very funny one,' his father frowned.

'So what did you think you saw tonight, Sophie?' Fleur asked.

'We saw a ghost standing by the headstone. All in grey, wasn't it, Jenny?'

Jenny nodded. 'Yes, a grey ghost. It stood, then knelt down by the head-stone. Then Sophie cried out and it vanished.'

* * *

It was quiet now, the children calmer, the parents puzzled, but reassured no actual harm had been done.

An hour later, Fleur and Jake were alone, the children tucked up asleep and the parents in the bar, mollified by a complimentary bottle of wine.

'Strange that the kids saw, or thought they saw, something, or somebody,' Jake said.

'I just hope it doesn't get in the papers. We don't need any more bad publicity. Poor Yvette, I must find out about her. Could there really have been someone there, in the copse?'

'Possibly an intruder, or maybe just the children's imagination. But one way or another, I think we should find out more.'

Fleur felt a warm glow at the *we*.

'I'd like to stay on here for a few days, do some digging, if you don't mind,' Jake said.

'That would be great. The garden cottage is free after the weekend.'

'I'll have to check back home, my grandfather's not well, and I still have some business in town. I'll stay at the hotel for now.'

'OK.' Fleur was disappointed.

'But I'll be around, and we've all day tomorrow, remember. I'll pick you up around noon?'

Fleur nodded and walked to the door with him. 'Thanks again, Jake, and for explaining about Merton.'

'Then I'm forgiven?'

'Nothing to forgive.'

He put his arms round her. 'Good-night, Fleur, and please don't worry. You're doing a great job.' He kissed her on the cheek, hesitated, then found her lips.

To Fleur it was the most natural thing to kiss him back.

Jake's arms tightened around her, then he let her go. 'Tomorrow then.'

Fleur watched Jake go, saw him get into his car and drive away, then she closed and locked the door.

Jake drove slowly down the drive and stopped close to the bushes. He got out, very quietly closed the door and walked towards the copse.

★　★　★

Promptly at noon Jake called for Fleur. 'All quiet?' he asked.

'It seems to have blown over, but it is a worry.'

'Try to forget everything just for a

few hours. Daisy?'

'A party, and Wanda's in charge.'

'Fine. So enjoy the freedom.'

As Jake drove towards the coast, Fleur's problems slipped away.

She took in the lovely scenery and sunshine.

'Weather's due to break,' Jake said, 'storm's moving in.'

'Well, today's perfect and this summer has been wonderful.'

Jake stopped at a picturesque small port with a straggle of houses and a village square. He parked by a hotel with a terraced outdoor restaurant practically in the sea. 'Out or in?'

'Out, I think. It's a lovely spot, Jake. How did you find it?'

'A guy at my hotel told me about it. Local caught fish is their speciality, and after lunch we can walk along the cliff path to the next village.'

'Great, I love walking. I never had time to do much in London, and I'm too busy now at the Manoir.'

A young girl came to take their order.

'Fish just caught this morning,' she smiled, 'we do a mixed plate.'

'Lovely,' Fleur said, 'just right.'

'Glass of wine?' Jake asked.

'No thanks. I've a busy evening ahead.'

'Day off, remember?'

'I don't think there is such a thing in my job,' Fleur smiled.

'I do wonder, though, Jake,' she went on slowly, 'if I've done the right thing, the Manoir, I mean. There just seem to have been so many problems lately.'

'Well, you don't have to worry about any unwanted ghosts! After last night I checked the copse myself and there was no sign of anyone,' Jake said. 'Don't lose heart because of a couple of setbacks, Fleur.'

'You're right. And today is lovely. I'd almost forgotten what free time was like.'

'So let's enjoy it.'

* * *

229

After a delicious lunch of freshly grilled fish and tiny boiled potatoes, they set off along the cliff path. 'Beautiful.' Fleur took deep breaths of the salty air. 'I'd love to live near the sea, Ben said that . . . ' She stopped.

'We've a holiday home on the west coast,' Jake said, and took her hand. 'It's right on the ocean. I'd like you to see it one day.'

For a while they strolled in silence until Jake stopped by a grassy hillock. 'Let's watch the sea for a while. And Fleur, I'd like to talk to you.' He took her hand. 'You mentioned Ben. Can you talk about him? Your life together? Or does it upset you?'

'No, no, it's nearly four years since he died. He was an architect. I worked in London, too, in financial management, but we wanted a family, country living, maybe working from home.'

'Like Jane and Sam?'

'Exactly. But a year after we married, I was pregnant. We were about to move into our new flat and we'd arranged to meet there after work. I was so excited, we were going to plan carpets, curtains . . . I bought champagne, a takeaway . . . then, at eight o'clock, Ben phoned. 'Be there in fifteen minutes,' he said.' Fleur swallowed. 'He never got there. It . . . it was a hit-and-run. The next I saw of Ben was his body at the hospital.'

'Oh, Fleur . . . ' Jake put his arm round her. 'A terrible time.'

'It was, but there was Daisy, you see. I had to keep going for her. She's nearly four now, and I have the Manoir. I'm lucky. Really.'

'No family at all? No distant relatives?'

'No, no family. My mother died when Daisy was a year old, but I have to tell you, Jake, Ben, my first and only love, will always be in my heart and he will always be Daisy's father.'

'Of course.' He pulled her closer and his lips brushed her hair. 'But you must know how I feel about you. I love you, Fleur. I knew that on the stairs that day in London. I had to find you, and now I have, I can't let you go. I want to marry you.'

Fleur never forgot that moment, the sunlit sea, the soft caressing breeze, Jake's arms around her and his lips soft on her hair. 'Marry me?' she whispered.

'Marry you. I love your courage, your tenacity, all the things you are, your beauty, the way you laugh, the way you are with Daisy . . . '

'Daisy! There's Daisy!'

'Of course there is. Who could possibly ignore Daisy? I want to love you both.'

'But . . . '

'You don't need to say anything. You just need to know I love you. And I understand so well about Ben.' His eyes clouded.

'Tell me,' Fleur said softly.

He sighed. 'First love, very, very painful, the loss . . . '

'Someone . . . died too?'

'No. Well, in a way. Casey, my first love . . . we were students at college. I thought we had a perfect love, then

Casey decided I wasn't enough, she needed more. She . . . she crashed into the fast life and never came out of it.'

'Oh Jake, that's awful.'

'She's a wreck, mentally and physically. In fact, she's in one of our homes.'

'But surely she'll recover?'

'I don't think she will.'

'Oh Jake . . .'

'Fleur, I only told you about Casey to show you I do know just a little about lost love, although I couldn't possibly compare it with you and Ben. And Casey, that was a long time ago, nearly ten years.'

She turned towards him. He kissed her and Fleur knew she was in love, truly in love, with Jake Merton. But there was Daisy, the Manoir, all her plans for the future, Tim and Celeste, Stefan and Wanda. She stared out to sea as though to find an answer on the sparkling horizon.

'Fleur, there's no pressure. I'll wait, and hope, but I had to tell you what's in my heart.' He kissed her again, and hand-in-hand they walked back towards the car.

★ ★ ★

They drove back to the Manoir in silence, both occupied with their own thoughts. Occasionally he touched her arm as if to reassure himself she was really there.

At the Manoir, guests were already on the terrace anticipating the evening cocktail hour.

'I must go, I should be there on the terrace,' Fleur said. 'Thank you for a wonderful day.'

He kissed her. 'No need to say anything, not yet. I have to check what's happening at home, my grandfather is very poorly, but I'll be here for a day or so. Oh. and I'm going to do some research on the Remondins.' As she was about to leave the car he pulled her back.

'Don't forget, Fleur, I love you and I want us to be together.'

Before she could say anything, Aimee came running down the steps. 'Fleur, there's a phone call, a Robert Maynard. He's called several times. He sounds worried.'

'Thanks, Aimee, I'll take the call in the office. Daisy all right?'

'As ever. She's playing in the garden with her friends. Wanda's there.'

'Thanks. Are you free, Aimee?'

'Sure, I've finished my shift in Reception.'

'Could you spare a little time to socialise with the guests on the terrace?'

'Really? I'd love to. Thank you, Fleur.'

'Delegation, delegation,' Fleur reminded herself as she hurried to her office and picked up the phone.

'Hello, Fleur here. What's the matter, Rob?'

'Fleur, it's dad. We're here in Brittany. You know he's taken an apartment quite near the Manoir?'

'No! But why?'

'I think he's lost the plot. He's doing

no work, all he can think about is the Manoir. It seems to have become an obsession. He was there today. You weren't there, but your friend, Tim, was in the chapel with an architect who told Dad it was going to be converted to a holiday cottage.'

'Well, not for a while, but what's that got to do with Paul?'

'No idea, but that's why I came over a couple of days ago. A neighbour tells me he's worried too, Paul goes out wandering late at night. You haven't seen him, have you?'

'Not lately, and he didn't tell me he was staying nearby. He still rings up with silly offers for the Manoir.'

'Look, Fleur, I can't stay over here for much longer, I don't suppose you could . . . '

'Goodness, Rob, that wouldn't do at all. He really dislikes me, and there's not much love lost on my side, either. I'm sorry, but . . . oh heck, OK, give me his phone number. I'll phone him, then we'll see. I'll get in touch with you if anything happens.'

'It's these night time jaunts that worry me. He's an old man and he will carry a heap of money around.'

'I'll see what I can do, Rob.'

'Thanks, I really appreciate it. I can come over again in about a week or so, take time off work, sort the old man out. He . . . he's not all bad, Fleur. Years ago . . . '

'I don't want to know, Rob, but I promise I'll do what I can.'

'Thanks.'

Fleur put the receiver down thoughtfully. Night excursions? Living nearby? Shadowy figures in the grounds? Could the ghost the children saw have had anything to do with her stepfather, and if so, what on earth was he doing hanging about Yvette's grave?

Fleur's Worst Nightmare

Fleur decided to take a peek at Aimee's handling of the cocktail hour before Wanda fetched Daisy from her party. Standing well back, she could see Aimee was doing wonderfully well, a naturally accomplished hostess. Guests who were gathered round her were laughing, listening to her every word, one or two of the men following her around the terrace as she circulated.

Looking up, Aimee noticed Fleur, who gave her a grin and a thumbs up sign. 'Well done,' she mouthed, then her smile froze. The man just by the door leading on to the terrace — Fleur was sure it was Christopher Jones.

Swiftly she ran up the terrace steps. As she drew nearer, he turned his head and looked straight at her. Their gaze held for a couple of seconds and Fleur waved to indicate she was coming to talk to him, but just then one of the guests put a hand on her arm. 'Ah, Mrs Weston, just the person.'

'So sorry, I'll be straight back but I must just see someone . . . ' She ran towards the double doors leading into the house. Christopher Jones had been there a minute ago, but now there was no sign of him.

Fleur looked around, went into the house, but Mr Jones, if that really was his name, had disappeared.

Fleur was sure he was lurking around the Manoir to no good purpose. Could he possibly be connected with Paul Maynard? What had he said his business was? Restoration and renovation? She dashed into her office, called up Google on her computer and typed in, 'Christopher Jones, Property Consultant, Hampstead, London.' Obligingly, Google produced half a million Christopher Joneses, but not one at the address he, whoever he was, had given.

Fleur stared at the screen. Could there be a connection between Mr Bogus Jones and her stepfather? After all, both were in property, both were hanging around the Manoir. Or was she just being paranoid?

'Mummee, Mum, look,' Daisy came running in to her mother. 'I got a party bag,' she announced, and tipped the bag on to the floor and sat down beside it.

Fleur knelt down. 'Did you have a nice time?'

'Mmm . . . look,' Daisy held up a little charm bracelet for Fleur's inspection.

'It's lovely. Everything OK?' Fleur asked Wanda, who had followed Daisy into the office.

'Fine,' Wanda replied. 'It was quite a big party with lots of children Daisy's age.'

'When's my birthday, Mum, can I have a party?'

'Of course you can. We'll need to invite all your friends. You've more friends here than in London, haven't you?'

Daisy nodded her head vigorously and gave a big smile. 'I like it here.'

Fleur hugged her tightly, 'Well we're not leaving at any price.' Suddenly she thought of Jake, his proposal, his declaration of love, the future he promised. But Jake was American, that's where his home and family were, so where would she and Daisy fit in?

'All right if I go help Stefan now?' Wanda asked.

'Of course, and thank you. Oh, and Wanda, how are the wedding plans?'

Wanda shrugged, and sighed. 'Big trouble, big decision. I and Stefan want the wedding here, but the families want it in Poland.'

'Well, they would, surely,' Fleur smiled. 'So why not have a ceremony in Poland and a party here at the Manoir? Invite anyone in your family who wants to come to stay.'

Wanda smiled broadly. 'An excellent idea. I'll tell Stefan.'

* * *

Next day, Fleur met Tim and his architect friend, Gerard, to discuss the plans for the chapel's conversion to a holiday cottage. She had been reluctant to commit herself, but Tim's enthusiasm for the project and a promised cash involvement from his father had persuaded her to go ahead.

When Tim and Gerard arrived, Tim gave her a big hug. 'Fleur,' he said, 'guess what? Yesterday, while you were out with Jake, Gerard and I were looking around the chapel and I can't wait to show you. It was Gerard who found it.'

'Found what?'

'Wait and see.'

As they went towards the chapel, Fleur's heart sank. Paul Maynard's car was in the drive and he was by the chapel door, trying to get in. When he saw Fleur, Tim and Gerard, he swung round. 'Fleur, hello. I . . . er . . . visiting . . . ' he tailed off.

Fleur was shocked by his appearance. Usually smart, even dapper, always in a suit and tie, he now wore jeans and a stained sweatshirt, his hair was too long and he was unshaven. 'Paul, what are you doing here?'

'Can we have a chat?'

It was the last thing Fleur wanted, but she'd promised Rob she would to try to help his father. 'I'm busy right now,' she said, 'but maybe this afternoon.'

'We've plans to convert the chapel to a holiday cottage,' Tim broke in, 'so we'll be a while here.'

'Convert?' Paul turned to Fleur. 'But I offered to buy it. You can't do this!'

'Of course she can,' Tim said sharply. 'It's her property, she can do what she likes with it. She has the right.'

'No!' Paul's face was suffused with rage. 'She can't, she has no right! No right at all!' He shouted, and stood in front of the chapel door, arms outstretched.

The three of them looked at him aghast.

'He's crazy,' Tim said under his breath.

'Paul,' Fleur said quietly, 'you can see we're busy. I'll phone you later, maybe come and see you. Leave me your address and phone number. I promise I'll ring you when we're done here.'

'I'll pay you double what he,' Paul indicated Tim, 'offers.'

'It's not like that, Paul.' Fleur was beginning to feel sorry for her stepfather, he looked so different from his usual confident self.

'Look, it's best if you go,' Tim said, and, for a moment, Fleur thought her stepfather was going to strike him.

'Please, Paul,' she said quickly.

He blinked and dropped his arms, stared at them for a few tense moments, then pushed past them and walked to his car.

★　★　★

'What on earth was all that about?' Tim frowned.

'I don't know,' Fleur sighed, 'but he seems obsessed with the Manoir.'

'Well, he's gone now, so let's get on with our survey.'

Tim opened the chapel door and switched on the main light. Fleur looked around, then she saw a space behind the altar where the doors had been. 'Where are the doors?'

'I hope you don't mind, but we needed to see what was behind them. Come and look.'

'You've been here before. I came the other day, there were footprints,' Fleur said.

'No, we only did this yesterday. Look.' Tim led the way through the gap where the doors had been and Gerard switched on a flashlight. 'Be careful, there are some steps.'

The air smelt damp and stale, and the darkness was oppressive. Tim took Fleur's hand. 'Tread carefully, it's a bit slippery.'

'Where does it lead?' Fleur peered into the darkness.

Now both Tim and Gerard had powerful flashlights working. Tim shone his on a blank wall straight ahead.

'That's it?' Fleur said. 'Another wall?'

'It's a wall, but there's a room behind it. Gerard's equipment tells him it was dug out a long time after the chapel was built. We need to break the wall down. I didn't want to do it without your permission, and it'll take some hefty machinery to shift it. Whoever built the cellar didn't want anyone easily gaining entrance.'

'So what do you think is behind the wall?' Fleur asked.

Tim shrugged. 'No idea, but we'll have to break through anyway if we're going to convert the building.'

Fleur shivered. 'Let's go back. It's cold down here, and a bit spooky.'

They went back up to the main chapel. 'Can you tell how long the wall's been there?' she asked.

'Probably, with the right equipment.

That is, if you are going ahead with the project?' Tim looked enquiringly at her.

'I don't know, Tim. Let's go back to the house, look at the plans. That cellar, I don't know . . . there's something about it . . . '

'Come on, Fleur, it's just a cellar, a place to store things.'

'So why hasn't it got a door?'

'I can't answer that, but I'm sure there's nothing sinister about it. Anyway, let me show you Gerard's plans.'

Fleur was glad when they were out in the warm sunshine, though storm clouds were beginning to build on the distant horizon.

Over a snack lunch they discussed Gerard's plans for the conversion and Fleur had to admit they were stunning. She looked out over her lovely gardens and couldn't envisage ever leaving here. 'All right, Tim, if you're sure about the money, go ahead,' she stated decisively.

'Great! But I can't start just yet. I've loads of work here already and of course there's my wedding.'

'After the wedding, then.'

★ ★ ★

Although it was late September, the Manoir season was still in full swing. It had been a busy day, and Fleur hadn't had time to contact her stepfather. By early evening, her conscience was pricking her, so she phoned him. There was no reply, so she left a message.

There was a message for her on her mobile, from Jake.

'Day spent on Remondin research — a big surprise. I'll call you tomorrow. Fleur, I love you.'

Her heart skipped a beat as she read the three words that mattered. 'Oh Jake . . . ' she said out loud, then thought, America? Leave the Manoir? She shut out the thoughts and went to find Daisy for their pre-bedtime hour. Rain was already drumming on the windows, the wind was rising fast and the sky was a threatening black.

While Daisy watched her favourite T.V. programme, Fleur went down to the drawing room to greet the new guests. She also wanted to check whether the mysterious Mr Jones would show up. He didn't, and she began to wonder whether she'd dreamt last night's appearance. She went back upstairs. A flash of lightning and a thunder roll made Daisy snuggle up to her mother.

'Don't like it, Mummy.'

'Don't worry, love. You know what my mum used to say to me, 'It's only angels moving God's furniture around'.'

★ ★ ★

Once Daisy was asleep, Fleur went to her office to tackle the endless paperwork, but it was work she enjoyed, especially when she could see an ever increasing healthy balance sheet.

Ever tighter, the Manoir was binding her to her new life, a life so much more satisfying than her life in London. But Jake? Her hand crept to her phone, she needed to hear his voice, but the only answer was from his message service.

Fleur worked on. The storm had passed but the wind was still howling round the house. Around midnight, she left her office and went to her room. Daisy was fast asleep. Fleur quietly slipped into bed and was asleep herself within seconds.

But her sleep was strangely troubled, and in a dream, old Mr Simkins was trying to tell her something. He had his clipboard, making notes over Yvette's grave, and was now kneeling down by the headstone trying to erase the words . . .

'No, don't!' Fleur shot upright and knew something was dreadfully wrong.

The night was no longer dark, and a red glow outside brought her running to the window. She heard a dreadful crack that wasn't sheet lightning. With a growing sense of horror, she saw that the chapel was on fire and the strong winds were blowing the flames towards the house. Between the chapel and the house was a large wooden shed where tools and garden equipment were kept. She could see that would go up at any second.

'Daisy, Daisy, get up, get dressed, I must raise the alarm!'

Outside, she ran into Stefan. 'Fleur, I've rung the alarm.' As he spoke, the fire alarms started clanging, and guests appeared at bedroom doors, tousled, sleepy, then instantly alert.

'Quickly, everybody out, on to the lawn.' Fleur was already ringing the emergency number. 'Stefan, go upstairs, make sure everyone's out. I'm ringing the Fire Brigade. Hurry, HURRY.' She went back to her room, where a sleepy, scared-looking Daisy was at the door. Fleur picked her up. 'Quickly, Daisy, go to Wanda, she'll take care of you. I must go and get Mr and Mrs Johnson out. They're on the third floor, not very mobile, and very deaf. Go to Wanda.'

'OK.' Daisy, hugging her teddy, went towards Wanda.

Fleur raced upstairs to room 10. When she burst in, she found the old couple fast asleep. 'Mr and Mrs Johnson . . . quickly . . . fire . . . hurry.'

It seemed to take an age before the couple realised what was happening. Mrs Johnson was trying to help her husband. 'Arthritis, he's very slow, Mrs Weston.'

Fleur found slippers by the bedside. 'These'll do . . . fast as you can.' She tried to speak calmly, but she could see the flames were about to reach the house, and part of the chapel roof had fallen in.

She shepherded the Johnson's down the stairs with smoke already drifting through the house. 'Nearly there, and I can hear the fire engine in the distance.'

Once outside, Fleur could see the chapel was well alight. The firemen had their hoses trained on it and jets of water began to shoot towards the flames.

Fleur ticked off names. Everyone was safe! She breathed a sigh of relief.

'All accounted for?' Wanda came over to where Fleur stood.

Suddenly, and simultaneously, a look of terror distorted their faces.

'Daisy! Where's Daisy?' Wanda cried.

'I thought she was with you!' Fleur said, fear in her voice.

They both raced to the house, only to be stopped by a fireman. 'Can't go in there, too much smoke.'

'My daughter!' Fleur screamed, fighting to free herself from his grip.

'We'll get her. Don't worry, the house isn't in much danger yet.'

'YET!' Fleur broke free, only to be stopped by another fireman by the door. 'We'll get her. Our crew are already in there.'

'But you don't know where she is, she'll be frightened!' and as Fleur spoke, a fireman came out of the house, wearing breathing apparatus.

'Daisy!' Fleur shouted.

'She's not in there.' He took off his

mask, 'There's no-one in there.'

'She must be! She must!'

'Fleur . . . ' There was a voice behind her, then she was in Jake's arms.

'Oh, Jake, it's Daisy. She must still be in there!'

Then a voice came from the crowd. 'Mummy, Mummy!'

Fleur spun round. There was her beautiful, precious Daisy, smiling and unharmed in the arms of a tall man.

The man came closer and held out the child to Fleur.

Fleur snatched her away. 'You!' she said, 'how dare you! Give me my daughter, and leave, this second. You've been hanging around here; up to no good; did you start this fire?'

'Fleur,' Jake said, as Daisy began to cry, 'Fleur, you're making a mistake.'

'Christopher Jones indeed!' She ignored Jake, clasping Daisy to her. 'Just go, right now and don't dare set foot here again, or I'll call the police!'

The man dropped his hands in a helpless gesture, gave one agonised look at Fleur and Daisy and turned to go.

'No,' Jake called out, 'Tony, come back. Fleur, he's not Christopher Jones. He's Tony Weston. WESTON, Fleur.

'Tony Weston is your father and Daisy's grandfather.'

A Plea For Forgiveness

On one level Fleur was aware of her surroundings; she even registered a faint dawn streak in the dark night sky. She smelt the smoke, heard the firemen calling to each other, the concerned conversations of the guests on the lawn. On another level, time was suspended and she was only aware of Daisy in her arms, and Jake with his hand on the tall man's shoulder.

It was only when Daisy struggled out of her arms and went across to the stranger and took his hand that, for Fleur, the world snapped back into place.

'This nice man found me. I was lost, and he brought me back,' Daisy said.

The man looked down at the little girl. 'She was a bit frightened, she'd left the house and wandered off into the copse. She was very brave, not crying at all.'

Fleur shook her head, something was very wrong. 'What did you say, Jake, just now?'

'I said this is Tony Weston, your father. I met him this morning at the records office. I've spent the entire day with him. He has a great deal to tell you, if you'll allow him.'

'My father? But . . . '

A fireman came across to Fleur. 'Mrs Weston, isn't it? You're the owner here?'

'Yes, I am. Thank you for coming so quickly.'

'Fortunately we're not far away. Your guests can move back into the house now. It's still quite smoky and some of the ground floor rooms are a little water damaged, but that's about the extent of it.'

Fleur snapped out of her trance-like state. 'Stefan, Wanda, can you man the kitchen? Hot drinks, food, whatever anyone wants. I'm so sorry everyone,' she told her guests.

'Not your fault, dear . . . '

'Excellent fire drill . . . '

'Good tale to tell back home . . . '

They straggled back into the house, chatting and talking together, united by their experience.

The stranger, Tony Weston, hung back. Daisy was still holding his hand. 'I rescued Teddy, see . . . ' In her other hand, she held her favourite soft toy. 'You coming in?' she asked the man.

He looked at Jake, then at Fleur, but said nothing.

'Jake,' Fleur said, 'what's going on?'

He put his arm round her. 'Trust me, let your . . . let Tony come in. I think you'll regret it if you don't. And, Fleur, he is your father.'

Just then, Tim and Celeste appeared. 'Fleur,' Tim said, 'what . . . oh no, the chapel!'

'Can we help?' Celeste asked.

'Yes, that would be kind. Some of the older guests are a bit shocked.'

Celeste and Tim both looked curiously at the stranger who was holding Daisy's hand.

'Have you seen the chapel, Tim?' Fleur said hastily. 'That's where the main damage is.'

'How did it start?'

'The fire officer suspects it was deliberate.'

'The little one's nearly asleep,' Celeste said, 'shall I put her to bed?'

'That would be a help. Go with Celeste, Daisy, love, I'll be up later.'

'Man come too.'

'No!' Fleur said sharply.

'Goodnight, then, Daisy.' The man disengaged his hand. 'Perhaps I shall see you in the morning.' He knelt down beside her. 'And perhaps you can show me your garden.'

'Yes, please,' Daisy smiled.

'My pleasure,' he said quietly, his voice choked with emotion.

Fleur deliberately shut out Jake's bombshell news. There was too much to do in the present without dealing

259

with spectres from the past, if indeed this mystery man *was* part of her past.

* * *

Grey dawn gave way to bright morning before all the guests had been settled, or resettled if their rooms had been smoke-damaged. Comparative calm descended on the Manoir by noon, but the firemen were still at the chapel site.

'Still some tests to do,' The chief fire officer was in Fleur's office, 'But I'm afraid it looks like arson. All those boxes and papers you had in there made it very easy for the fire raiser. But it's a good strong building, stone built, no wooden pews. The main damage was the roof. I should get your insurers here as soon as possible, if I were you.'

'Thank you so much, you and your men have been tremendous.'

'All in a day's, well, night's work, Mrs Weston. I . . . suppose you don't know of anyone who would want to cause you harm?'

Paul Maynard sprang immediately to Fleur's mind, but surely even he would never deliberately put their lives in danger. 'No,' she said firmly, 'I can't think of anyone.'

As the fire officer went out, he bumped into Jake and Tony Weston. Fleur's heart sank, she didn't want to face Jake and the stranger — and stranger was the only way she could think of him.

Jake kissed her. 'Where's Daisy?' he asked.

'She slept late, then Wanda took her to the beach.'

Just then Aimee came into the office. 'Fleur, Rob Maynard on the phone in Reception. Do you want me to transfer his call?'

'No. Just tell him we're all OK and I'll phone him back as soon as I can.'

Jake turned to Fleur. 'Why don't you sit down and hear what Tony's got to say?'

Fleur looked Tony Weston full in the face for the first time and caught her breath. Daisy! Something about the eyes, an expression . . .

'I met Tony at the records office, we were both after the same thing, Remondin history,' Jake started to explain. 'Tony knows a lot more than I'd ever find out. Well, he was married to a Remondin.'

Fleur glared angrily at Tony Weston.

'I never had a father! My mother coped on her own with no help from you at all. You abandoned us!'

'I didn't know about you, Fleur. Babette never told me she was pregnant. I found out much later.'

'So why didn't you help then? We had very little money. Mother had to sell off things from the Manoir. Oh, I can't listen to you . . . ' She stood up.

Jake held her arm. 'Please, Fleur, sit down. Your father,' he emphasised the words, 'made every effort to help. He wanted to come back, he sent money, but it was always returned.'

'But, Jake, he left my mother for someone else. It broke her heart.'

'I can't deny that,' Tony Weston said, 'and it was the biggest mistake of my life. And I've paid for it . . . for that dreadful infatuation.' He closed his eyes, the pain reflected in his expression.

'So, if that's all it was, infatuation, you could have come back. So why didn't you?' Fleur said, but not quite as sharply.

'Oh, Fleur, you must know the world better than that. Babette had rejected her family, the Remondins — for me! And I was an Englishman. For her there was no going back.'

'But . . . all those years . . . '

'I had a very long spell in hospital where all I wished for myself was to die.' There was a strained silence, only broken by Aimee coming in with some coffee. Quickly she set down the tray and left.

Jake poured out three cups.

'So why are you here now?' Fleur said.

'To make amends, if you'll let me. I

didn't mean to say anything to you, then I met Jake and he persuaded me that I should at least make myself known to you. Then there was the fire, and Daisy.'

'But I can't forget my poor mother. All those years of struggle, then a rotten second marriage. And it was your fault!' Fleur was near to tears.

Tony Weston sighed, 'It's no good, Jake, I told you. I'm only distressing Fleur. I can't do that to her. I'll go.'

'No,' Jake said, 'wait.' He went to sit next to Fleur and took her hand. 'Remember, Fleur, at the restaurant by the cliff, how you said you wished for a family, how alone you sometimes felt. Well, now there is someone, your family, your own flesh and blood. I know your father has hurt you. He knows it too, and he's asking for your forgiveness, Fleur, and a second chance. Look into your heart. Can you truly reject him?'

'I never meant to come back,' Tony Weston said, 'I only meant to watch from a distance. But now I've seen you and Daisy . . . ' He stopped, too near to tears to carry on.

There was a long silence. Fleur was aware of outside noises, vacuuming, a murmur of voices, the phone ringing. She looked at Tony Weston, her father. All these years he had been waiting, on the outside, and now . . . well, now what?

Daisy suddenly burst into the room followed by Wanda. 'Mummy, see, these seashells are for you. Oh, and for the nice man, too.' Carefully she selected a small conch and held it out to Tony Weston. 'Put it in your ear, and hear the waves,' she ordered.

He did so and smiled. 'I hear the sea.'

Daisy took his hand. 'Now you can come and see my garden.'

Tony Weston cast an agonised look at Fleur.

The silence seemed to last for ever, then Fleur spoke. 'That's all right, Daisy, you go with . . . with your grandad.'

'He's my grandad? I've got a grandad!' whooped Daisy. 'That's a good thing to have, isn't it? It's what all my friends have.' And she put her hand in Tony's and led him out of the office.

At the door, he turned. 'Fleur,' his voice choked, 'thank you, thank you so much.'

★   ★   ★

'Well done, Fleur.' Jake took her in his arms and kissed her.

'Could someone tell me, please, what's going on?' Wanda asked.

Fleur smiled. 'I'll explain later. Right now, I need to look at the chapel.'

'I think Tim's over there now with Gerard,' Wanda said.

While the main house was relatively unscathed, the chapel, the main target of the arsonist, if it was arson, was quite badly damaged; the roof timbers were burnt, the building open to the sky. A fireman was hosing down the walls, steam rising as he did so.

'Fleur,' Tim picked his way over, 'what a mess. But at least now there's a clear way to our hidden storeroom. The fireman says it shouldn't be too difficult to get into it. He says to wait until tomorrow. He's got someone coming to inspect the damage and only then can they let us in.'

'Oh well, it's been shut up for so many years, another day won't matter. There's plenty of clearing up still to do in the house,' Fleur said.

'Are you all right, Fleur?' Tim looked concerned.

'It's just . . . I've had a bit of a shock. That mystery guy I told you about . . . well, turns out he's my father.'

'Your father? Really? Well, that's great!'

'But all these years I've hated him for what he did to my mother.'

'Fleur, from what I've seen of him,' Jake said, 'I'd say your dad was one of the good guys. He made a mistake, of course he did, but he's trying so hard to make up for it now.'

Before Fleur could reply, her mobile rang.

'That was Rob, Rob Maynard,' she told Tim after the call. 'Paul, my stepfather, has collapsed, he's been taken to hospital. Rob's on his way over here. He's in a terrible state.'

'Isn't he at the hospital?' Jake said.

'He's been there all morning, with the police.'

'Police?'

Fleur nodded. 'It seems that Paul has confessed to starting the fire.'

A Problem Solved

When Rob arrived, Fleur called for strong coffee and took him into her office.

'How could he, Fleur? How could he put lives at risk? He has his faults, but this . . . '

'Everyone's safe Rob. No-one was hurt.'

'After he started the fire, he went straight to the police and gave himself up. He told the police he had a right to the property, told them you refused to sell, so he thought it best to burn the place down, then no-one could have it.'

'Oh Rob, how dreadful. But have you any idea why he wanted the Manoir so desperately?'

'I didn't, but I do now.' Rob took a gulp of coffee. 'I hate to say this, Fleur, but my father married your mother for just one thing — the Manoir.'

'But why? He's rich, he has properties abroad, an art collection worth a fortune.'

'It wasn't about the money, Fleur. It's about what he hopes to find in the cellar of your chapel.'

'How can he possibly know what may be there?'

'Dad has lots of European contacts throughout the art world. After World War Two, there were rumours about hidden caches of treasure trove. The Germans had access to French museums and art galleries and as the tide of war turned in the Allies' favour, they began to move treasures from major cities to unlikely venues like the Manoir de Belvoir, a run-down country house, hoping to return at some point in the future to reclaim them.'

'You're saying there's treasure trove in our cellar and that's what Paul's after?'

'Yes, I think so.'

'But it could rightfully belong to anyone, and certainly not to the Remondins.'

'It would be difficult to prove ownership after all this time. It might be a case of finders keepers.'

'So why set fire to it now?'

'Who knows? He maybe meant to scare you off and things just got out of hand. I don't think he's truly rational any more.'

As Fleur was digesting this news, Jake came into the room.

'Oh, Jake, this is Rob Maynard, my stepbrother. Rob, this is Jake. He's American,' she added unnecessarily.

'Oh — Rob. So your dad is . . . ?'

'Paul Maynard, yes.'

'Right. Well look, sorry to butt in, but Tim's at the chapel site, he wants to break into the cellar. There's quite a crowd over there.'

Fleur jumped up. 'We must stop him. We'll have to get the police. Rob, will you fill Jake in while I go on ahead?' And Fleur set off at a run towards what was left of the chapel.

When she reached the building, there was a group of people standing around, Tim and Gerard at the front, ready for the firemen to give the word to go ahead.

'Tim! Stop!' Fleur cried.

'Fleur! What's the matter?'

Briefly, she told him Rob's story.

'Wow. So wartime loot could be in there?'

'Possibly. And it doesn't belong to us. I'm going to phone the police.'

'Once this gets out, the press'll be on to it like locusts. What a story! And you won't ever have to worry about financing the Manoir.'

'Tim! That stuff in the cellar probably isn't mine.'

'I didn't mean that. I meant that the story would generate lots of interest in this place.'

'No, Tim, I don't want to be that sort of tourist attraction.'

'Too late.' Jake and Rob had joined them and Jake pointed to people coming up the drive, most of them armed with cameras. 'I'll head them off. I should call the police right away, Fleur. They'll rope off the area and leave a guard until whatever's in there can be moved to a secure location.' He walked down the drive and spoke to the crowd. After a few minutes, they turned away and left.

'Thanks, Jake. What did you say?'

'That it wasn't safe, that there may be explosives left over from the war. Well, it's the truth in a way, there could be some pretty explosive stuff in there.' He put his arm round Fleur. 'Cheer up, Fleur, this could be the scoop of the year.'

'I don't want that. I just want my plain old Manoir.'

Jake kept his arms round her, kissed her and held her close.

Rob gave a discreet cough.

'Sorry, Rob.' Jake released Fleur. 'And I'm sorry about your father.'

'Any point my going to see him at the hospital?' Fleur asked.

'Not really, he's off in his own little world.'

'Look, we'll sort everything out, and when Paul's well, maybe I could help.'

'Thanks, Fleur. Now, I'd better check with the hospital. I'll ring you.'

Fleur kissed Rob on the cheek, then hugged him. 'You're my family, Rob, we must spend more time together.'

'I'd like that Fleur.'

After he'd left, Fleur took a deep breath. 'I seem to be acquiring a set of relatives, Jake, a family, at long last.'

★ ★ ★

Within hours the police had cordoned off the chapel site. Press interest had been diverted by Celeste, and the police arranged to break into the cellar late the next evening.

They had rigged up temporary arc lights, which cast a deep shadow as they worked on the entrance to the cellar. It didn't take long, a final sledgehammer blow, a crack, and the wall fell inwards in a cloud of dust. There was a gaping black hole, a rush of stale air. Tim shone a flashlight into the cellar, Rob's beam criss-crossed his and a policeman added his. No-one spoke as the lights showed up packing cases, wooden crates and pictures encased in protective hessian. The air was damp and cold. Fleur shivered.

'Now what?' Tim said.

'Mrs Weston, we'll seal this off again and you'll want to bring the experts in,' the policeman said.

'Shouldn't we take a look?' Tim was eager.

'No.' Fleur was firm. 'I don't want anything to do with it. There may be things in here belonging to my family, the Remondins, but I just want to hand it all over to the authorities. This has caused enough heartache.'

★ ★ ★

Back in the house, Tim asked, 'Paul obviously knew about the cellar, so why didn't he just break in before you came to live in the Manoir, Fleur?'

'It was rented out, remember. I think he panicked when my mother left it to me. And I'm sure it was Paul I saw once or twice in the night. There were lights on in the chapel, someone in the grounds, and I shouldn't be surprised if he wasn't responsible for the slanderous newspaper articles.'

'And wasn't he hanging around Yvette's grave? Scaring the children? Why should he do that?' Tim frowned.

'I might have an answer,' Tony Weston said. 'In my search for Babette, who I didn't know had died, I found press reports blaming the Remondins for not accepting Yvette as Raoul's bride. She was from the south of France, the unoccupied zone, and there was a lot of ill-feeling about that, as you can imagine. Raoul, the last of the male Remondins, was a war hero, and he knew about the cellar. I believe he wrote to Yvette and entrusted the secret to her. These family letters eventually came to Babette. After her death, Paul read the letters and started on a quest for the hidden treasures.'

'Poor Yvette, poor Remondins,' Fleur said.

'But you've made this a happy place, Fleur,' Jake said.

'And I need to stay, to make sure it stays a happy place.'

'But Fleur,' Jake frowned.

Tim coughed discreetly. 'Best be going. I've to report back to Celeste.'

'And I must go to the hospital,' Rob said.

'Fleur,' Tony Weston was tentative, 'do you think . . . a room here . . . ?'

Fleur nodded. 'I can't forget the past, . . . but there's Daisy, she has a right to her grandad. Go to Reception. Aimee will fix you up.'

'Thank you, Fleur, so much.'

*　*　*

Jake and Fleur were left alone. He kissed her and held her close. 'Fleur, you know I love you, you know I want to marry you. Can't you put me out of my misery and say yes?'

'Jake, I love you too, you know that, but how can I leave the Manoir? There's so much more to do here and Daisy, she loves it so. I can't just abandon it.'

He was silent for a while, then he kissed her again, almost despairingly. 'My home is in America and I'd gladly leave it for your sake, but my family depend on me. My grandfather's very old and frail and my father really needs me.

'I want you, and Daisy to meet my family.'

'We can visit,' Fleur said desperately, 'commute.'

'Oh Fleur, I want my own home, my own family. I don't want to commute between Europe and California.'

'People do.' She was pleading now.

'I couldn't.'

For a few seconds they faced each other, then they were in each other's arms.

'There has to be a way. I'll go back to the hotel now, you've had a long day and too much has happened. Sleep on it. We'll talk tomorrow,' Jake said.

* * *

The next few days flew by in a whirl of activity. As well as the normal business of the Manoir, Fleur had to accommodate the police, followed by academics and war historians with research teams. Vans rumbled up and down the drive carrying away paintings, artefacts and cases of silverware and china.

It was Tony Weston who eased Fleur's burden to a great extent and she began to rely on him more and more.

Jake phoned, pressure of work took him to Paris. She didn't see him for a week and her heart yearned for him.

A couple of weeks after the fire the Manoir was back to normal and the chapel stripped bare. As Tim said, 'Just right for reconstruction and conversion.'

Rob brought news of his father. 'He's no better. I'll have to go back to London, make arrangements for his care there.'

The main summer season was nearly over, but Fleur was surprised by the number of advance bookings. Tim was right, the story of the chapel hiding wartime treasures was a magnetic draw. Now everything had gone for cataloguing and possible redistribution, the story could be told.

* * *

Fleur went to pick some of her vegetables and found Daisy and Tony Weston immersed in a plan for the coming year. 'See, Mummy, Grandad's marking out a big plot, he's drawn a plan too — t'matoes, salads . . . '

'Oh, that's far too large for you, Daisy.'

'Georges says it OK and Grandad'll help.'

'Fleur,' Tony Weston got to his feet, 'I

didn't mean . . . oh dear . . . Daisy, can you help Georges for a few minutes? I want to talk to . . . er . . . Fleur.' He beckoned her to a nearby bench. 'Fleur, I've no right at all to interfere, you can tell me to shut up any time, but I do hate to see you so unhappy.'

'I'm not,' she protested, 'I'm just busy.'

'It's Jake, isn't it?'

'No!' There was a long pause. 'Oh, all right. I miss him so much, Dad.'

Tony Weston's heart soared. She had called him Dad. 'Fleur, I've ruined my own life, I threw away your mother's love, don't you do the same; you'll regret it forever. You love Jake, don't you?'

'I do, so much, but the Manoir, how can I leave it?'

'Look, Fleur, there is a possible solution. What if I run the Manoir for you? Stefan's got plans for his cookery school, Tim for his chapel conversion. I could hold it all together. I know I don't deserve it but please, Fleur, it would give me a purpose.'

Fleur hung her head.

'Fleur . . . Fleur, dear, please don't throw away the love that Jake has for you.'

She lifted her head, her eyes streaming with tears.

'What's wrong?' Tony said in alarm.

She threw her arms round his neck. 'Thank you, thank you, Dad. That's just what I needed to hear.'

* * *

Fleur didn't anticipate being married quite so soon, but Jake's grandfather was gravely ill, and the family wanted him to return to America immediately.

'I have to go home, my grandad . . . ' he told Fleur.

'Oh Jake, I'm so sorry.'

He took her hands. 'Fleur, I've told my family about us, could we be married in California by special licence? Grandad's set his heart on it.

'He knows he's only a short time left and he so wants to meet you.'

Fleur didn't even have to think about it. 'Alright, Jake. I'll talk to Dad and Daisy, they'll be fine staying here. We can have a big party later. You book the flights and I'll pack.'

Tony Weston was delighted to step into his managerial role so soon, and Daisy was placated with a firm promise of a trip to Disneyland later.

A few days afterwards, Fleur and Jake were married at the Merton family home in San Diego, with Jake's grandfather in attendance.

After a brief honeymoon in London, they flew back to Brittany, and Jake made his base at the Manoir.

Tim and Celeste planned to marry in the new year so there was a triple wedding celebration to plan for. Fleur closed the Manoir for a week at Christmas for a truly international celebration for the three happy couples; herself and Jake, Tim and Celeste, Wanda and Stefan. Friends and families; British, French,

Polish and American, descended on the Manoir, and on a day of sparkling winter sunshine the guests sat down to a banquet featuring international cooking on a splendid scale.

★ ★ ★

Many speeches and toasts later the young members, well wrapped up, walked off the lunch in the Manoir's grounds.

'You've made this such a happy place, Fleur,' her friend, Jane, said.

'Yes, it seems to be working out. Stefan and Wanda, Tim and Celeste, are all part of the Manoir now, and my dad's taken to it wonderfully well. I'm sure Babette would be happy.'

'I'm cold,' Daisy said, just as a bell clanging from the house announced afternoon tea.

'I couldn't eat another thing,' Fleur groaned.

'We could! Mince pies! Christmas cake!' and Alice and Daisy ran off towards the Manoir.

Jane shivered. The winter sun had long gone and the dusky air was chill.

'Coming for log fires and hot punch?' Sam was already running after the children and Jane followed, but Jake held Fleur back.

'You're truly happy?' he asked. 'With me and the Manoir?'

Fleur kissed her new husband tenderly. 'Our future's before us, Jake, and as long as we're together, you, me and Daisy, that's all my happiness.'

And as they walked, arms around each other, back through the garden, a bright new moon rose in the night sky and illuminated their pathway back to the Manoir de Belvoir.

THE END

Books by Joyce Johnson
in the Linford Romance Library:

SUSPICIOUS HEART
EDEN IN PARADISE
SWEET CHALLENGE
FOREVER IN MY HEART
TWISTED TAPESTRIES
ALL TO LOSE
CUCKOO IN THE NEST
ROMANTIC LEGACY

We do hope that you have enjoyed reading this large print book.

Did you know that all of our titles are available for purchase?

We publish a wide range of high quality large print books including:
Romances, Mysteries, Classics
General Fiction
Non Fiction and Westerns

Special interest titles available in large print are:
The Little Oxford Dictionary
Music Book, Song Book
Hymn Book, Service Book

Also available from us courtesy of Oxford University Press:
Young Readers' Dictionary
(large print edition)
Young Readers' Thesaurus
(large print edition)

For further information or a free brochure, please contact us at:
Ulverscroft Large Print Books Ltd.,
The Green, Bradgate Road, Anstey,
Leicester, LE7 7FU, England.
Tel: (00 44) **0116 236 4325**
Fax: (00 44) **0116 234 0205**

THE ORANGE MISTRESS

Sara Judge

Alice Wingard tells the story of how
Nell Gwyn saves her from destitu-
tion when she is orphaned. Nell
takes her to live in a bawdy house in
Coal Yard Alley. The well-educated
Alice finds her new surroundings
shocking. Yet the girls' friendship
deepens as, together, they move on
from the theatre in Drury Lane, to
Pall Mall and then to the court of
the lascivious Charles II. Sharing
happiness and sorrow, they encounter bloodshed, passion and political
intrigue . . .